Emily,
I hope you enjoy
this!   Craig

Jacob
OF AVONDALE

P. CRAIG PACKER

Jacob
OF AVONDALE

TATE PUBLISHING
AND ENTERPRISES, LLC

Published by Tate Publishing & Enterprises, LLC
127 E. Trade Center Terrace | Mustang, Oklahoma 73064 USA
1.888.361.9473 | www.tatepublishing.com

Tate Publishing is committed to excellence in the publishing industry. The company reflects the philosophy established by the founders, based on Psalm 68:11,
"The Lord gave the word and great was the company of those who published it."

Book design copyright © 2012 by Tate Publishing, LLC. All rights reserved.
Cover design by Kenna Davis
Interior design by Christina Hicks
Illustrations by Charlotte S. Packer

Published in the United States of America

ISBN: 978-1-62024-201-8
1. Juvenile Fiction / General
2. Juvenile Fiction / Fantasy & Magic
12.05.09

DEDICATION

For Charlotte, my own real-life Princess Catherine, and
for Hailey, Anna, and Preston, my true and living heirs, to
whom I bequeath the beautiful Kingdom of Avondale.

I wrote this book for you.

ACKNOWLEDGMENTS

There are many people to thank for their help in bringing this book to fruition.

Thank you to a whole host of my early readers—a few of whom never returned the stack of paper I often referred to as "my book." Special thanks to those who boosted my confidence by telling me you couldn't put it down and read late into the night, despite angry and sleepy spouses annoyed by the bedside lamplight. I even thank those who spent weeks and weeks slowly—and I mean slowly—savoring every single sentence while I nervously waited for a word or two about whether or not you were enjoying the book. You all know who you are.

Thank you to Charlotte, Hailey, Anna, and Preston—my biggest devotees—Mom and Dad for supporting me, and to all of the people at Tate Publishing for helping to make this book the best it could be.

I would like to apologize to all of the patients of mine who not only suffered through their dental appointments but were forced to listen to me discuss this book incessantly as I held them captive with needle and drill.

Lastly, to my Heavenly Father who listened as I prayed for help to see this through and inspired me when I needed Him to.

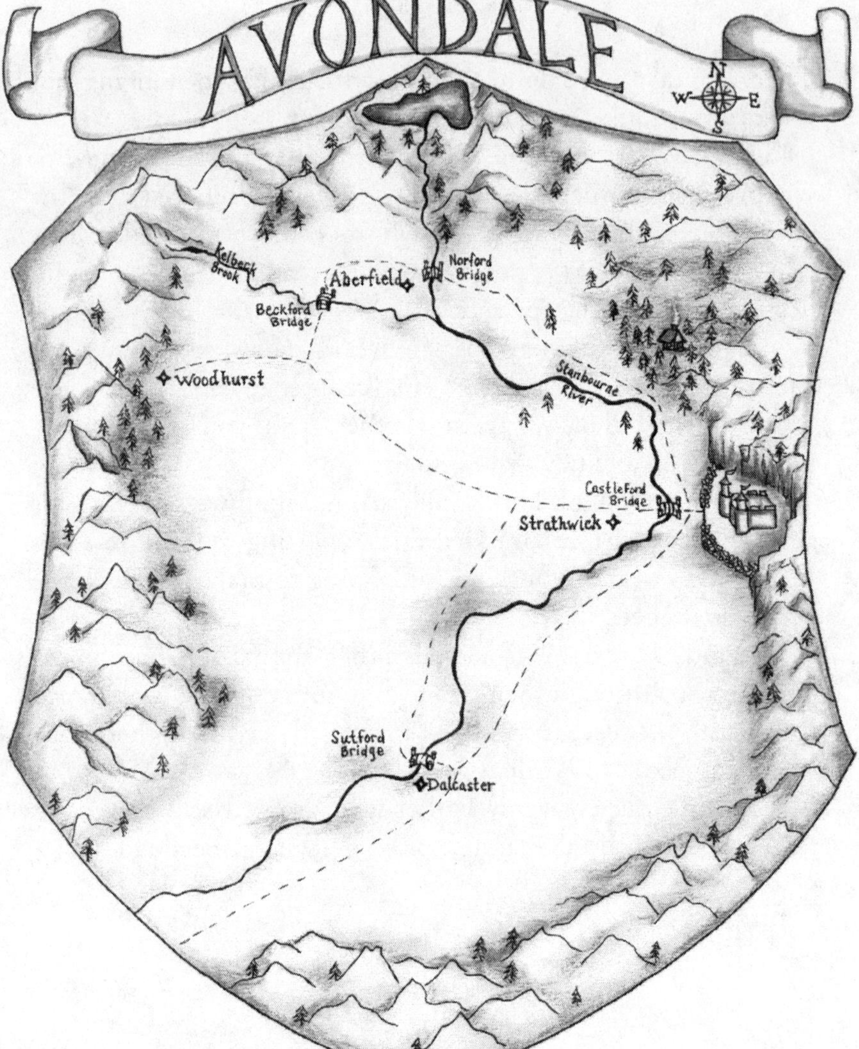
AVONDALE
N
W
E
S
Kelbeck Brook
Aberfield
Norford Bridge
Beckford Bridge
Woodhurst
Stanbourne River
Castleford Bridge
Strathwick
Sutford Bridge
Dalcaster

WORD MEANINGS

PREFIXES AND SUFFIXES

Avon: river

Aber: mouth of a river

Beck: stream

Bourne: stream

Caster: fortification

Dal: meadow by a river

Dale: valley

Ford: crossing

Hurst: hill

Kel: spring

Nor: north

Ock: oak tree

Stan: stony

Strath: vale, valley

Sut: south

Tarn: lake

Wick: settlement

PART I

AVONDALE

CHAPTER 1

"You pick that up right now!" echoed the queen's voice from down the long, dimly lit hallway as she disappeared around the corner.

"Yes, Your Majesty," was Jacob's only reply.

What he wanted to say was, "Pick it up yourself, you old hagfish!" But as many times as he thought about talking back to her, he knew that he never really would. He was afraid of the "consequences." The "consequences" on the bottom floor of the castle—the ones with the bars, the chains, and the filthy drinking water. So, as usual, Jacob bit his tongue and did exactly as he was told. The most infuriating part was that the queen was to blame. *She* would never see it that way, even though she had just come barreling around the corner, knocking Jacob flat on his back. The tray of food that he had been carrying was now scattered all around him.

Queen Millicent had been moving very quickly for someone of her tremendous size. *She must have been off to something very urgent,* Jacob thought. "It's not very often that Her Royal Hugeness passes up a meal, even if it *is* all over the castle floor."

When he heard the stifled laughter coming from a small room a few feet away, Jacob realized that he had spoken out loud. He recognized the laughter immediately and smiled broadly.

"Catherine, what are you doing in there?" Jacob picked himself up from the floor and dusted himself off with his hands.

The royal princess of Avondale stepped out into the hallway. "Hi, Jacob, I was hiding from my mother. One of my boring princess lessons is supposed to begin soon. I heard what you called her." She tried unsuccessfully to suppress another laugh.

Jacob blushed with embarrassment. Catherine had that affect on him quite often.

The princess was a beautiful young woman with long, dark hair and a smooth, soft complexion. She was slender and graceful, which was surprising considering the wide girth of her mother. Jacob was all too aware that the princess had the ability to weaken his knees when she smiled that flirtatious smile. It was something about her deep, brown eyes and the way they sparkled when she looked up at him. He wasn't sure if she looked at everyone that way or if they had something special between them—he didn't dare ask.

When they were children Jacob and Catherine had spent most of their days playing together in the castle or on the royal grounds. Catherine's favorite game was hide and seek, and she won nearly every time. Jacob liked it best when she would pretend to be a princess and he a knight, off on some amazing and exciting adventure. They also enjoyed running through the beautiful castle gardens and searching for insects, frogs, and other small animals. Jacob longed for those days before they had both grown up and been given responsibilities. He was an orphan and a servant. The king and queen had taken him out of the orphanage while he was just an infant and raised him to do their bidding.

Catherine, on the other hand, was royalty and was expected to behave as such. The queen would often remind her that princesses don't catch frogs and grasshoppers, and they surely don't spend their days playing with servants. She was now a little over seventeen years old, and Jacob was closer to nineteen, although nobody knew his real birthday.

Over the years, Jacob had grown into a tall young man. Doing various castle chores and taking care of the royal horses and stables had made him physically fit and strong. He didn't know if he was handsome, but even if he was he knew it wouldn't matter. He was only a servant. He knew that he needed to try and put aside his feelings for Catherine, but he found that difficult to do, even now as he looked at her and she gave him that powerful smile.

"I'm sorry to talk about her like that. I know that I should be grateful for everything that she and your father have done for me." Jacob had fond memories of growing up with Catherine and with the other servants in the castle, but the king and queen had never been very good to him.

In fact, Queen Millicent's husband, King Humphrey, was even worse than the queen herself. He was a short-tempered man who loved the power provided by his crown and his throne. He spent most of his time ordering servants around, hunting animals throughout his kingdom, or just sitting in his royal chambers with his one and only friend—the court jester.

"Don't worry. I would never tell her what you said. And besides, you were right—she doesn't very often pass by a hot meal without taking a bite or two."

Jacob smiled. "Thank you. I'd better get this cleaned up. I still have to finish my inside chores, feed and exercise the horses, and clean out the stables. And the jester is probably wondering why I'm taking so long with his breakfast."

"I'd love to help, but you know how the queen feels about that. Besides, I have that lesson down on the main floor. I'm supposed to learn how to perform a proper curtsy that is fitting of a princess. Doesn't that sound fascinating?" She rolled her dark brown eyes.

"I understand," Jacob said with a smile. "I'll see you at supper time."

"I hope so." Catherine glided down the hallway.

Jacob quickly picked up the scattered food and tried to make it as presentable as possible. He had no intention of going all the way back down to the kitchen for another plate. He hurried up the straight staircase to the top floor of the castle where he knew he would find the court jester waiting in his cramped yet well-adorned quarters.

Jacob had always found it odd that nobody seemed to know the jester's actual name. In fact, in all the years that he had been in the castle he had only heard the unusual little man referred to as "the jester."

"Fetch me the jester," King Humphrey would bellow, or "Jester, recite me my favorite bard this instant!"

The jester would immediately comply—whether out of respect for the king or fear of the consequences, Jacob could never really tell. As different as the two of them were, there was a connection between them that Jacob had stopped trying to figure out.

As Jacob reached the top of the staircase with the tray of soiled food in hand, he heard a strange whispering coming from the room near the far end of the hall. In all of the years that Jacob had been a servant in the castle, he had never seen the inside of that room. In fact, not only was it always closed, but there was a very large lock on the door at all times. Jacob often wondered what had been hidden away so carefully, but he assumed that he would never see inside the mysterious room. Now that the door was open and there was noise coming from inside, he couldn't help but sneak quietly down the hallway to see what was happening.

Every footstep seemed louder than the last, and the corridor was long. Eventually, Jacob arrived at the open doorway and carefully peeked inside. He saw the court jester standing near the far wall with his back to the door. The little man seemed to be profoundly captivated by something and was whispering in an eerie, monotone voice.

Jacob glanced around the room and saw many exquisite pieces of armor, tapestries, swords, shields, vases, and numerous other old and ornate items. As Jacob studied the room, out of the corner of his eye he noticed the jester move slightly to his left. Turning his attention back toward the jester, Jacob saw something that nearly made him drop the tray of food once again.

On a shelf not ten feet away was an old human skull, and in the middle of its bony, white forehead was a large, oval-shaped gem. It was a deep, dark blue that was almost black in the dim light of the room. Jacob was instantly fascinated by the skull and wondered how it could have been prepared so intricately to allow the gem to fit so perfectly. Wanting a better view of the skull, Jacob leaned slightly to his right. His weight shifted beneath him, causing the wide wooden floorboard under his foot to creak noticeably. Quickly jumping backwards away from the doorway, Jacob pushed the flat of his back against the stone wall, wishing that he could make himself thinner than he really was. He nervously held his breath, expecting at any moment to be discovered.

The jester's incantation, however, never ceased and less than a minute later, Jacob mustered the courage to look back into the forbidden room.

The little man, who still had his back to the door, was no longer speaking in a whisper, and although his words were now loud enough to hear, Jacob still couldn't understand them. It was a language that he had never before heard. *Is this some sort of enchantment?* Jacob wondered. The jester raised his voice even louder and began flailing his arms about wildly. After another minute or so, however, he finally stopped his chanting, dropped his head, and sighed deeply.

Jacob turned his attention back to the strange skull before him, and suddenly some invisible force powerfully seized his mind. The priceless gem seemed to be calling out to him, and he felt an intense desire to dash in and take possession of it. As he peered into the dark, empty eye sockets of the mysterious skull, Jacob made up his mind. Setting down the tray of food, he prepared to step through the door and rush toward the skull.

"What in the king's name are you doing here?" the jester yelled angrily as he turned around and faced Jacob. He stepped to his side, intentionally blocking Jacob's view of the shelf behind him.

The skull's sudden disappearance and the roar of the jester's voice tugged Jacob's mind back to the present. "I…ah…just um… brought you your food," answered Jacob nervously as he picked up the tray and held it out in front of him as proof.

"You know better than to look in here!" yelled the red-faced little man. He quickly stepped out of the room and slammed the door closed behind him. Then, reaching into his tunic, he withdrew a large ornate key that was attached to a surprisingly thin gold chain and quickly locked the door. After replacing the chain around his neck, he grabbed the food tray and said, "Get away from here this instant, and tell nobody what you have seen or there will be—"

"I know," Jacob interrupted. "There will be consequences."

Jacob turned to walk down the hallway toward the long set of stairs. Glancing back over his shoulder, he saw the jester take the food tray into his room down the hall from the mysterious door.

As he descended the long staircase he thought, *I need to get back into that room, and I don't care about the dungeons that lie beneath the floors of this castle.* As he pictured the skull in his mind, Jacob again felt a powerful longing to obtain the magnificent gem—no matter the consequences.

CHAPTER 2

Throughout the rest of his day as he tried to focus on his work, Jacob could not shake the thoughts of the strange skull from his head. In fact, later on, when he found himself in the king's stables, he realized that he didn't even remember doing his inside chores. Jacob was so consumed by what he had seen in that locked room on the top floor that he had carried the king's linens to the washroom, cleaned out the king's chamber pot, and swept the guards' rooms without even noticing that he had done so. Now that he was in the stables he was able to think a little more clearly. Maybe the memory of the morning's events was fading, or perhaps it was because he enjoyed being around the horses. Whatever the reason, Jacob was able to focus a little better on the task at hand.

After spending an hour or so brushing, feeding, and giving water to each of the horses, Jacob realized that the dreaded time had arrived. There was only one horse in the whole stable that he disliked spending time with, and today was the day that he was supposed to ride her—Queen Millicent's own chestnut-brown mare. Both she and the queen were equally intimidating. This horse was not only very big and strong but actually seemed to have the queen's personality. Jacob had often thought that if Millicent herself were a horse, she would be a fatter version of this one.

The mare, however, was perfectly suited for the queen since most of the royal horses would buckle under her tremendous weight. In fact, when Queen Millicent *did* try and mount her horse for a ride into Strathwick or along the countryside, it would take the help of five or six of the king's royal guards to push her into the saddle. It was no wonder that she rarely attempted the matter. Nonetheless, it was important that the horse was always fit and strong, and it was Jacob's duty to see to that.

After putting off the inevitable ride for as long as he could, Jacob pulled the mare out into the courtyard. He took a deep breath, put his left foot in the stirrup, and with much effort tried to swing his other leg up and over the saddle. As usual he found it quite difficult.

I'm a tall, fit young man, thought Jacob. *If anyone should be able to mount this horse easily, I should.*

Using all of his effort this time, he positioned his left foot into the stirrup, grabbed the reins with his hands, and pushed hard off the ground with his right leg. Although it nearly exhausted him, Jacob finally managed to pull himself up into the saddle. As he looked toward the ground he felt as if he were looking out of a window on the second floor of the castle.

"My, you are a big girl," Jacob said as he patted her on the side of her neck.

The mare reared back and jumped to one side, but when she realized that Jacob wasn't falling off any time soon, she trotted off toward the outer castle wall. Jacob knew that the mare would rather run free and untethered, but she accepted his presence with reluctance and set off on their usual route.

CHAPTER 3

Elizabeth watched the princess try to curtsy for the fifteenth time and tried to subtly gesture to her to straighten her back a bit more. She'd been working with Catherine for weeks during their lessons and at times wondered if she'd ever turn this young woman into a royal princess.

"No, no, no!" the queen yelled. "You're doing it all wrong!"

"I'm sorry," the princess apologized. "I just can't seem to get it right. I guess my heart just isn't really in it today."

"She has come a long way in a very short time, Your Majesty," Elizabeth said. "Please have patience with her."

King Humphrey, who was sitting at the far end of the room, bellowed, "We never should have let her play with that blasted servant boy!" Under his breath, he said, "She acts more like a commoner than a princess." Even the king didn't like to stir the wrath of his behemoth bride.

"Elizabeth, need I remind you that you are being paid handsomely for your services, and in return I expect great results. There are other private tutors in Avondale, you know," Queen Millicent threatened.

"Yes, Your Majesty," Elizabeth said. She wished, at times, that she would have never applied for the job to tutor the princess. In fact, she almost turned down the position after being interviewed by the royal couple a few months earlier. Elizabeth had expected that any child who had grown up in this castle would be as ornery as the king and queen. It was at that time, however, that Catherine entered the room and kindly introduced herself. Elizabeth saw her exquisite beauty and her kind demeanor and decided instantly to accept the job and become her tutor. *If for no other reason,* Elizabeth had thought, *I must try and shield this extraordinary young woman from her parents' verbal attacks.*

"Let's try it one more time," Elizabeth said kindly. "It is really a simple thing to bob a proper curtsy. Remember that a princess should do a nice simple curtsy where you nod your head and bend your knees at the same time. Do not overdo it by bending too deeply."

"Okay, let's go over the steps once more, and I will try and concentrate this time," Catherine promised.

"All right, here are the steps. From a standing position with your arms at your sides, gently hold your skirt on both sides with your thumbs and first two fingers, pinkies extended. That's great. Now at the same time bend and cross your left leg behind your right one."

Catherine intently watched her kind tutor and mirrored her every move.

"That's superb! Now make sure that your toe is touching the floor while you are bending your right leg slightly. Wonderful! Keep your back straight and hold your head in the nod. That was perfect! Great job that time."

"Except for the fact that it should only take about two seconds!" hollered the queen as she rolled off of the sofa and awkwardly rose to her feet. "Here, watch *me* this time."

Just as the queen began her attempt at the curtsy, the king screamed, "No, Millicent, remember what happened the last—"

King Humphrey's sentence was cut short by the sound of a thunderous crash. At first no one realized what had happened, but as they all ran over to where the queen had been standing just a few seconds earlier, they found her sprawled out over the top of a pile of fabric, stuffing, and splintered wood. Apparently, just as the queen attempted the part where she was to cross her left leg behind her right, she had lost her balance and fallen backward onto the chair behind her.

"Well," the king said, sighing. "At least it was only a chair. Last time she tried something like that we had to find a new cook."

CHAPTER 4

As Jacob and the mare approached the gated stone archway that served as the entrance and exit to the royal grounds, the guard on duty swung open the heavy iron gate to let them pass through.

"Try and enjoy your ride today," said the sturdy guard.

"I'll try, Ossian," Jacob replied. "Although I'm sure you've seen my companion for the afternoon."

Ossian had always been kind to Jacob. He was a strong man of above-average height. His most noticeable feature was his dark, well-groomed mustache that curled up slightly at each end. It matched the dark wavy hair on his head that was always parted perfectly on the left side. He had a strong jaw and light brown eyes. Above those eyes were two bushy eyebrows that came dangerously close to touching in the middle. Ossian took his guard duties seriously, even though there had been no serious threat to the castle or the king and queen for as long as Jacob could remember.

"I'll be back at my usual time," Jacob said. "Just before supper is served."

"I will be here to open the gate as always," Ossian replied.

Jacob nodded his thanks and glanced back over his shoulder to view the royal castle of Avondale. Despite his dislike for the current king and queen, he had to admit that they lived in a wondrous place. The castle itself was built on a small hill and had a stately appearance. Its position on the hill allowed its occupants—and more importantly, the royal guards who were stationed as lookouts in the battlements and towers—to look down to the west and survey the surrounding area with ease.

It was also perfectly situated for protection against the elements and attackers since it backed up to tall, sheer cliffs that led up to a large forest-covered mountain range. As the mountain sloped downward on both sides of the castle, it formed a sort of cove that protected the castle's sides from any possible attack. Because of its proximity to the cliff, most of the royal grounds and beautiful gardens were located between the main castle doors and the outer castle wall.

Jacob turned back around and looked directly west. Just up ahead he could see the Stanbourne River and the Castleford Bridge that spanned its width.

The kingdom of Avondale was a lush valley that was bordered to the west, north, and east by thickly forested mountains. Through the valley the meandering Stanbourne River flowed from the north to the south. It originated from a high mountain lake far to the north called Lake Ocktarn and was joined by a smaller, spring-fed stream called Kelbeck Brook in the northern part of the kingdom. Jacob had heard that one of the kingdom's villages, Aberfield, was located at the confluence of these two rivers.

Two other cities were also situated along the river's edges as it passed through the valley. Strathwick was nestled near the center part of the valley a few miles west of the castle, and Dalcaster was located in the southern part of the kingdom. After passing by Dalcaster, the river turned to the southwest and headed away from King Humphrey's realm. To the northwest of Strathwick at the eastern edge of the western forest was a village called Woodhurst. The townspeople from these four settlements, and many other isolated farms and cottages scattered throughout the countryside, were the people of Avondale, and much to their dismay, King Humphrey was their crowned ruler.

Over the years, Jacob had heard whisperings about the previous ruler, King Rowland, who had apparently died suddenly from illness nearly two decades earlier. The people seemed to be quite fond of the previous king. There had been peace and prosperity during his short eight-year reign, and he was a kind ruler who didn't overtax or overburden his people. Above all, it was said that he was a fair and honest man. After illness took his life, King Rowland's first cousin, Humphrey, took the throne and has ruled ever since.

Humphrey was a lazy monarch with an appetite for gold and expensive apparel and food. Taxes quickly increased, and people knew that the consequence for even the slightest offense was time in the royal dungeons. The people of Avondale soon learned that although many were banished to those wretched prison cells, very few, if any, ever came out.

No one seemed to know what happened to the previous queen, Queen Mary. After the tragic death of her young husband she attended the royal funeral and was never heard from again. She had always been the quiet type and had kept to herself most of the time. In fact, she was so rarely seen outside of the royal grounds during the days of her husband's reign that most of the citizens of the kingdom didn't even know what she looked like. The few people who did know her well, however, said that she was kind and gentle and very much in love with her husband. The older castle servants had often told Jacob how nice it was to work for the previous monarchy.

A few days after the funeral, King Humphrey and Queen Millicent paraded themselves through the valley as they moved from their estate in Dalcaster to take up residence in the royal castle.

Jacob and the mare turned to the north and began to follow the road that led toward Aberfield. Lightly kicking his heels, Jacob urged the horse into a fast run, and the stubborn mare reluctantly agreed. Although she hated to comply with Jacob's wishes, she was glad, it seemed, to get out for a run along the countryside.

Aberfield was approximately two day's journey by horse along the road on which Jacob now traveled. He had never been there personally, but he had heard from a few of the castle servants that it had been, at one time, a charming little town. Many times while exercising the horses along this road, Jacob dreamed of riding straight to Aberfield and leaving the servant life behind him. He knew, however, that he could never really leave. It wasn't his fear of being caught and punished, as much as the fact that if he left he would never see Catherine again.

After a few hours of riding, with an occasional break to walk, Jacob and the mare reached the usual turnaround point. Not only was this location just the right distance from the castle to adequately exercise the horses, but it was also a very peaceful and secluded area. The forest and the stream came close together here, and there was a large rock along the river's edge that was perfectly shaped for resting against. There was also plenty of water and vegetation for the horses to replenish their spent energy.

Jacob pulled back on the reins, stopped the mare, and carefully slid out of the saddle. After checking the location of the sun in the sky, he realized that they had arrived in almost half the time that it took most of the royal horses.

"I've got a new appreciation for you," he said to the mare as he sat down and leaned against the smooth boulder for a brief rest. "You may be stubborn and ornery, but you are an amazing horse."

The mare ignored Jacob completely and walked over to a patch of long green grass and began to graze.

Placing his hands behind his head, Jacob looked up at the bright blue sky. It was a pleasant spring afternoon, and the sounds of the river behind him and the rustling of the forest leaves relaxed him and unclouded his mind. As he usually did at least once each day, he tried to remember his parents. He had fragmented memories of smiling faces looking down on him, and he thought he remembered kind, gentle eyes and tender expressions of love. Yet Jacob never could recall any physical features long enough to form a recognizable face. He realized, as much as he hated to admit it, that he just couldn't remember his parents and that he would never see them again.

A growl from Jacob's stomach interrupted his meditation. He usually took the time to pack a light meal for these afternoon excursions, but the events earlier that morning had disrupted his usual routine and he had forgotten.

"We should get back now," Jacob said as he pushed himself up from the rock and began walking over to where the mare had just been grazing.

To Jacob's surprise, however, the horse was no longer there. Worried, he attempted a weak whistle—he never was very good at that—and called out to the mare, but he heard nothing in return.

How long was I daydreaming? he thought as he checked the position of the sun in the sky once again. It hadn't been too long, it seemed.

Jacob didn't know what concerned him more—the thought of walking all the way back to the castle or having to tell Her Hugeness that he had lost her prized horse. As his despair mounted, he noticed that he was just able to see the big mare's hoof prints in the soft earth. King Humphrey's crest was stamped into the horseshoes of all the royal steeds, but the size of these prints made them unmistakable.

Jacob mumbled, "There aren't many horses in this kingdom with a hoof like that." He quickly followed the tracks and saw that they led directly into the thick forest. "This can't be good."

CHAPTER 5

Princess Catherine preferred eating her meals in the castle kitchen whenever she could get away with it. She was much more comfortable eating and conversing with the cooks and other servants than she was with her mother and father. She knew that during supper she was required to join the king and queen in the formal dining room. Catherine was expected to practice her table manners, be inconspicuous, and only eat small portions. "Princesses are not pigs!" the queen would say.

"And yet my mother's a mammoth," Catherine would occasionally reply under her breath. Luckily the dining room table was so long that with her seated in the middle, neither of her parents could hear her from where they sat on each end. In fact, the whole meal was rather comical—the king and queen would shout back and forth to each other. It usually went something like this:

"Humphrey, dear, could you please pass the roast chicken?"

"Of course, my queen!" the king would yell back to her as he rang the bell to summon a servant. Moments later, a servant would appear from the door behind him, and the king would instruct him to take the roast chicken to the queen. The servant would do as commanded and then leave the room.

"Millicent, would you please pass the bread and butter?"

"I'm sorry, Humphrey, but I am afraid there isn't any left. However, could you spare some Yorkshire pudding?"

"Yes, dear," the king would shout as he rang the bell to summon the servant again.

"My queen, please send down the applesauce."

"It seems to have been finished, dear," she would shout back with a muffled voice while licking the bowl clean.

This would go on and on until, by the end of the meal, all of the serving dishes would be piled on one end of the table, the servant would be physically spent, and the king's and queen's voices would be completely hoarse. To top it all off, Catherine was always still hungry.

It was no wonder that Catherine enjoyed her peaceful meals in the castle kitchen. As she sat there now, enjoying her dinner, she spoke with the cooks and other servants. Many of these servants had worked in the castle since the days of King Rowland and Queen Mary. Catherine was always full of questions about those days, and the servants, it seemed to her, were always full of carefully worded answers.

"Blythe, how long have you been the queen's seamstress?" the princess asked as she looked at the kind woman sitting across from her.

"It must be coming up on twenty-seven years now, my dear. I served Queen Mary for nearly eight years, you know," the old woman responded.

"So you must have been here the day I was born then," said Catherine matter of factly.

"Um, well, yes…I suppose I was." Blythe gazed downward to avoid making eye contact with the princess. "Well, that's it then, back to work," she quickly added as she jumped out of her seat and left the kitchen.

After a brief moment of odd silence and exchanged glances, the rest of the staff jumped to their feet and began doing their various chores. The conversation had definitely come to an end.

Whatever secret they're keeping, they aren't very good at it, the princess thought. She left to continue her studies, determined to find out what they weren't telling her.

CHAPTER 6

Jacob had never ventured into the thick, dark woods before this time. He had heard that the people of Woodhurst were quite comfortable with the dense forests of Avondale, but to Jacob the sights and sounds were foreign and mysterious. The forests were home to wolves, bears, and small wildcats, along with other animals such as boar, deer, and various types of rodents and birds.

"Not to mention all of the insects," mumbled Jacob, as he walked by a very large spider busily spinning a web between two trees.

Jacob wished that he had brought along a sword or a bow to protect himself from any possible predators. In fact, he had an intense desire to turn around, leave the forest, and begin the long walk back to the castle. He knew, however, that not only would he be severely punished for losing the queen's mare, but he would never make it back before nightfall without her speed. It was already late afternoon. Jacob trudged onward.

Shortly after entering the forest, the mare's hoof prints had vanished due to the thick undergrowth and fallen twigs and leaves. Walking slowly, Jacob searched for broken branches and listened for noises that might lead him in the right direction. After an agonizing period of time —it was probably only thirty minutes, but it seemed much longer to him—Jacob realized that he was lost. He tried to remember landmarks that he could use to find his way back, but the trees and other surroundings had all begun to look the same. To make matters worse, the dense canopy above blocked his view of the sun, preventing him from knowing which way was west toward the river valley.

On the verge of despair, Jacob smelled something. Instantly his stomach growled, and his mouth watered. He was hungrier than ever now, and as he glanced around, trying to discern which direction the tantalizing aroma was coming from, he saw a little wisp of smoke up ahead. Forgetting about his current predicament, Jacob scrambled up a small hill to his right, trying to get a better view of his surroundings.

As he crested the hill, he saw a small basin below, no more than two hundred yards away. In the basin's center was a quaint little dwelling with lazy, gray smoke floating from its chimney. Even from where he stood, Jacob could see two horses standing next to a small stable inside a corral not far from the cottage.

Jacob immediately noticed that one of the horses was much larger than the other. *I've found Queen Millicent's mare!* With a smile on his face and his mouth watering, he rushed toward the cottage as quickly as his legs could take him.

CHAPTER 7

Catherine had spent her last few hours unproductively. Every time she tried to concentrate on a task, her mind went back to the awkward silence in the kitchen earlier that afternoon. She had always felt that there was a secret that was being kept from her but never before had it been as obvious as it was today.

If only Jacob were here to talk to. He would know what to do, the princess thought. For some reason just thinking of Jacob gave her hope and an inner strength, and with a new sense of resolve Catherine stood up and walked out of her room—determined to get some answers.

Most of the time the king and queen could be found in the dining room or lounging around the royal quarters. Catherine decided to check the dining room first. As she exited her room, she headed straight toward the castle's grand entrance hall. Walking down the familiar wide hallway, the princess couldn't help but admire the tapestries, paintings, and statues in this part of the castle. She always found them intriguing. There were expensive artifacts and other decorative items located throughout the castle, but this grand entryway was especially well adorned.

As she passed by the guard stations—one on each side of the main entrance—Catherine reluctantly glanced up to view the two enormous paintings that had been hanging there for as long as she could remember. Every other piece of castle art was rotated and rearranged on a regular basis by strict command of the queen. These two paintings, however, hovered over the castle entrance at all times.

On the left was her father, King Humphrey, wearing his golden crown and a deep purple tunic made of fine silk. The king was noticeably younger in this portrait, but his physical features were unmistakable. Catherine had never liked the expression on her father's face in this painting. It was a smile, but it was unnatural and forced.

Hanging on the right was a portrait of Her Highness, Queen Millicent. She had a few less wrinkles and a little less gray in her hair, but other than that the queen was exactly the same. She too was wearing exquisite purple clothing, and her head was adorned with an amazing jewel-encrusted crown. The queen wasn't even attempting a smile.

Catherine had been embarrassed on many occasions as a guest or visitor came through the castle doors and gasped at the paintings. Realizing that they had gasped out loud and trying to correct their social mistake, most would say some thing like, "How exquisite!" or "Oh my, how...lovely!"

The king and queen would beam with delight and explain how expensive the paintings were and how they were forced to sit still for many agonizing hours while the best artisan in all of Avondale painted their likenesses.

Catherine shuddered at the sight of the paintings and looked away. Then, remembering her quest for answers, she began her search again.

Surprisingly, Catherine found that the dining room was unoccupied, so she headed toward the royal quarters located in the southeast wing of the main floor. As she approached the entrance to her parent's chambers, Catherine heard voices coming from the throne room directly ahead. Not wanting to interrupt, the princess quietly crept toward the open archway. Listening attentively, she recognized the voices as those of her father and the court jester in a heated argument.

"I already told you, I don't know how much he saw!" the jester said. "I don't think he was standing there for very long, but I cannot be sure."

"What were you thinking, leaving the door open like that anyway?" the king said angrily. "That room is to be locked at all times!"

"I usually don't leave it open, Humphrey, but I'd lost track of time. I tried two new incantations, and I still couldn't get the gem to even so much as shudder, let alone come out of that detestable skull. I don't know what else to try."

"There is nothing left *to* try!" the king said. "We have tried smashing the skull with a hammer and with a sword. We've tried prying the gem out of its forehead, and now you have tried using magic. It's indestructible! It won't even come off of the shelf. It feels as if it weighs as much as all of the gold in my kingdom. For nearly two decades we have been obsessed with that loathsome thing, and I for one have given up."

"Well, I haven't given up yet. There is magic and power in that skull—I can feel it. Why else would your cousin have it locked in its own room on the top floor? The rest of the treasures and heirlooms that Millicent keeps in there are worthless in comparison."

"You may be right," the king admitted. "But I fear we will never know. You had better hope that servant boy didn't know what you were up to—no one but Millicent and I know about your magic. That is only *one* of the secrets that must never be discovered."

Catherine quietly turned and tiptoed away. *Jacob and I need to talk.*

CHAPTER 8

Jacob was winded when he reached the door of the cottage. He was normally a cautious young man, but his excitement over finding the mare and the smell of food settling over the basin made him knock without hesitation.

When the door jumped open and Jacob saw the man standing before him, he wondered if he had just made his last mistake. The middle-aged man was large and strong and glared menacingly at Jacob as he ducked through the doorway, but what worried Jacob the most was the sharp, broad sword in the stranger's calloused hands.

Instinctively, Jacob took a step back as his mind raced for a solution to this new problem. Even though he was a strong young man, Jacob was inexperienced in fighting and swordplay, and this man was obviously skilled at both. To make matters worse, Jacob was weaponless. Although it meant leaving the queen's mare behind, he decided to make a hasty retreat into the forest.

"Sorry to bother you, sir," said Jacob as he continued to back away from the door. "I would rather take my chances with starvation and wandering than to quarrel with that blade of yours."

"A seemingly wise choice, young man," said the stranger as he stepped from the cottage toward Jacob. "However, you are just as likely to meet your ruin choosing the first as you are the second." The expression on the man's face softened slightly.

"That may be so, stranger, but I will take my chances with the forest creatures," replied Jacob as he turned to run.

"You are no stranger to me, Jacob of Avondale. Although I admit we have never met before."

Jacob stopped and turned back. "How is it so that you know my name yet in the same breath you confess that we have not met?"

Looking pleased, the man said, "My name is Raoul, and I will keep to myself how I guessed your name. I mean you no harm. You are welcome to a morsel of food, a wandering mare, and directions to where you want to go. We rarely have visitors here, and the sword is a precaution that I leave near the door."

Raoul leaned the sword against the cottage and motioned for Jacob to follow him through the doorway. Jacob, relieved that his life was no longer in jeopardy and that he would soon be filling his empty stomach, started toward the cottage door. As he walked by he glanced at the impressive sword that leaned against the wall and saw a crest on the hilt that looked vaguely familiar. The thought of the sword left as quickly as it had come as his stomach growled again.

Jacob was impressed when he stepped through the door and glanced around the small, well-built cottage. The walls were straight and square and made of timbers from the forest that had been carefully shaped and placed to fit together precisely. The door was sturdy and strong, and the windows were well placed to allow warmth from the sunlight to help heat the small cottage during the cold winter months. The roof had been painstakingly thatched with wheat straw and was watertight and resistant to wind. Jacob could see that there was a woman's touch at work within the cottage. The main room, which acted as a kitchen and an entryway, was clean and neat. Freshly cut wildflowers were centered on the table where Raoul motioned for Jacob to take a seat.

"It isn't much as far as dinner goes, but have a bowl of stew and a piece of bread if you would like." Raoul placed the food on the table in front of Jacob.

"That's very kind of you, sir," mumbled Jacob through a mouthful of hot stew. "I don't want to be rude, but I really must be on my way soon. I'm a servant in the castle, and will likely be punished for my late return."

"I was surprised when the tall mare arrived riderless. It seems that she may have left you intentionally." Raoul laughed.

"There's no doubt in that. That's the queen's mare, and she and the queen share their disdain for ordinary folk."

"Ordinary folk indeed!" Raoul responded more loudly than he intended. "Humphrey and Millicent were quite ordinary themselves not too long ago. How quickly one forgets the past when it's convenient."

"Is it better to know and forget then never to know at all?" asked Jacob softly.

"Well, young Jacob, the day is getting old, and the answer to that question would best be discussed on another day. Finish your meal quickly, and we will get you on your way."

Raoul and Jacob soon left the cottage and turned toward the horses in the corral.

"Can you point me in the direction of the river?" asked Jacob.

"If you would have me as your guide, I will lead you out of the forest. It's not far if you know the path, but it can take the rest of your life, however short it may be, if you do not. Besides, I have some questions to ask along the way."

"Your company and your assistance would be equally appreciated, sir," Jacob replied. "And you may ask questions, but I do not have many answers."

"Call me by my name, and I will do the same if it suits you," Raoul insisted. "We'll need to walk with the horses since most of the forest is thick with branches that hang down far too low to pass under while riding, especially a horse as tall as your mare." He led his horse toward a small opening in the trees ahead.

Jacob pulled the mare behind him as he followed Raoul. "How do you keep the pathway straight in your mind?" He squeezed the queen's horse between two closely spaced trees.

"I'll answer your question, if you promise me this—don't tell anyone of our cottage here or of the path through this forest. You are welcome to come alone at any time, but our existence here has been unknown for longer than you have lived, and I would like to keep it that way."

"I won't tell anyone your secret, but I *would* like to visit occasionally as I exercise the horses," Jacob answered. "I see very little of Avondale outside of the castle grounds, and kind friends are difficult to come by." *What would cause a man to live in such a secluded place*, Jacob wondered. *Has he offended the King?*

"You may come whenever you'd like. Now look at that small mark high on the trunk of that tree." Raoul pointed to a long slender pine just up ahead.

About ten feet off of the ground Jacob could faintly see a small oval-shaped mark that had been carved into the trunk. It was so inconspicuous that Jacob never would have seen it had Raoul not shown it to him.

"There's a mark just like that one every thirty feet or so. I've learned the way, after all of these years, without the marks, but my wife still finds them helpful on occasion. Part of the path up ahead follows a game trail for a brief while, but we have intentionally created our own part of the trail through a more dense section of forest," said Raoul as he continued leading his horse up ahead of Jacob.

The way was so narrow, and the trees around them so close, that the two men couldn't even walk beside their horses. Jacob followed behind Raoul's horse, keeping his distance from its powerful hind legs while continuing to pull and tug the queen's mare behind him.

"What is your wife's name?" Jacob asked. "And why wasn't she at home?"

"For now, I have questions for you. Maybe next time you visit I will be the one giving answers," replied Raoul. "We'll speak when the trail widens." The two men quietly walked single file through the dense woods. As conversing was too difficult to attempt, Jacob passed the time by looking for the oval marks that he found every so often along the trail. He noticed that as he passed by each tree that held the oval mark he was just able to locate the next one up ahead. He had the advantage of knowing in what direction to look, since Raoul was leading him, and he wondered if he would be able to return by himself at another time.

Eventually Jacob and Raoul reached the game trail that was used by the forest animals as they travelled to the Stanbourne River to drink. The trees thinned, and the two new friends were able to walk side by side.

"It's only ten minutes or so from here to the edge of the forest. Even though the path is now clear, I would still like to continue to walk along."

"The path may be clear, but I am new to the forest and would still appreciate the company," Jacob admitted, wondering if he sounded more like a boy than a man.

"Tell me, how did you find yourself a servant in the royal castle?"

"There's little to tell. I may have more questions than you do about my life, but I will tell you what I know."

As they walked, Jacob told Raoul about how King Humphrey and Queen Millicent had taken him from the orphanage in Strathwick when he was very young. He explained that the other servants in the castle had raised him from infancy and given him servant duties early in life.

Raoul listened intently without interrupting. He seemed quite interested in what Jacob was telling him, and at one time when Jacob paused briefly, Raoul simply said, "Tell me about Princess Catherine."

Jacob tried not to blush. He had intentionally not spoken of the princess up until now, not really sure how to approach the subject without conveying his feelings for her. He thought carefully about what he wanted to say, and how to word his answer. Raoul simply waited.

"The princess is a kind young woman, not at all like her parents in any way whatsoever," Jacob finally replied.

"So I have heard," Raoul said thoughtfully.

After a few minutes of walking in silence, the two companions reached the edge of the forest and stepped out into the open. The dirt road was just a few yards away, and the river was flowing gently just beyond it. They had exited the forest a few hundred yards north of where the mare had disappeared. Jacob glanced up at the sky and noticed that it was now quite late in the day. He needed to hurry home and sneak in without getting into much trouble with the king and queen. He would probably just make it before nightfall.

Raoul noticed Jacob's worried look and said, "Hurry home, but come and visit when you can."

"Yes, sir. I mean, Raoul," Jacob answered as he mounted the mare with some difficulty and turned southward toward the castle, speeding home.

As he had predicted, Jacob arrived at the castle wall just as the sun was setting. Once again the mare's tremendous speed and endurance impressed him thoroughly. Along the way he passed by a small group of peasants that were traveling northward toward Aberfield. Jacob rarely came across other people along this road, and he longed to stop and talk with the travelers. He wanted to learn about life outside of the castle and hear stories of people and events in other parts of the kingdom, but his tardiness had caused him to hurry onward.

A short time later, Jacob had been surprised when he saw a lone rider racing by in the opposite direction on a beautiful jet-black horse. The rider was a woman, judging by her attire, but she was wearing a hooded cloak and didn't look in Jacob's direction as she rode quickly by.

It is almost nightfall, and she travels alone many miles from Aberfield, Jacob thought. He was worried for her safety but quickly realized that she would soon reach the peasant group at the speed she was traveling. *She will join them for the night and be safe enough until morning.*

Now, returning home much later than usual, Jacob was worried about his own safety. Trying to make as little noise as possible, he slid off of the mare and walked quietly toward the stone archway that led to the castle grounds.

As he approached the gate, he heard a familiar voice say, "I have been worried about you. You're more than three hours late in returning."

"I'm sorry," Jacob whispered quietly. "The mare wandered off, and I had to search the forest to find her. Do the king and queen know that I am late?"

"I don't think so, but you had better hurry through anyway." Ossian slowly opened the heavy gate, trying to make as little noise as possible.

The gate's hinges made several awful groaning noises that seemed to Jacob to be much louder than they really were.

"I volunteered for the late watch also so that I would be the one to let you in when you returned," Ossian whispered. "The lookouts won't be a problem."

"Thank you. I don't know if my offense is strong enough for the dungeons."

"It depends on their royal moods, but it would've been worse to leave the mare behind."

The rusty hinges creaked again as Ossian closed the heavy gate slowly behind Jacob and the mare.

Jacob smiled nervously and said, "I'll be sure to oil those tomorrow after my morning chores are through."

Night was coming, and as the setting sun from the west cast an orange hue over the castle, it reflected off of the windows on the upper floor. Jacob saw no movement coming from anywhere near the castle or on the grounds ahead, but as he tiptoed through the courtyard, pulling the mare behind him, the mean-spirited horse seemed to know exactly what was happening. She pulled against the lead constantly, stomping her powerful hooves into the earth and whinnying loudly the whole time.

She even seemed to be smiling at Jacob when he looked back and hissed, "If I get in trouble, you can forget all about your trips outside the castle walls. You will be exercised on the walker or not at all!"

After what seemed like an eternity, Jacob reached the stables, gave a big sigh of relief, and stepped through the tall doorway. "Let's get you to bed," Jacob said to the mare.

"You're late!" came a voice from behind Jacob.

CHAPTER 9

Jacob froze for an instant but quickly realized that he had heard the voice of the princess. Turning around, he replied, "Catherine, you nearly scared me to death. I was expecting to be caught by the king or queen."

"I'm as mad as they would be. Maybe even more!" she said in return. "I've been worried that you had been robbed or injured by falling off that horse. What kept you so long?" she asked as she furled her brow. It seemed to Jacob that she was trying her best to look more furious than relieved.

"The mare wandered off into the forest when I stopped for a rest. It took me quite some time to find her."

"I don't like that you ride alone each week. I'll ask my parents if I can go with you next time. How's that for a punishment?"

"I might prefer the dungeons, but the punishment seems to fit the crime," Jacob answered with a wide grin.

Trying not to smile herself, the princess replied, "My mother will probably argue, but I can explain to her that a proper princess needs to practice graceful horsemanship. That should convince her. Now, onto other matters—we need to talk."

Luckily, at this time of night King Humphrey and Queen Millicent were often sitting down for a second supper. When they were immersed in their extravagant meals, the royal couple was rather clueless as to the happenings inside the castle. They were completely oblivious about Jacob's late return and hadn't even noticed the princess's pacing about and many trips to the stables that evening. Jacob and Catherine were quite safe from interruption as they sat in the drawing room recounting the day's curious events.

"And then when I asked Blythe if she was here the day I was born, she got completely flustered and ended the conversation. It's obvious that they all know something they aren't telling me."

"So what did you do?" asked Jacob, hoping that it would soon be his turn to talk.

"I decided to ask my parents a few questions, but when I went looking for them, I overheard a conversation between my father and the jester. I think they were talking about you."

"About me?" questioned Jacob as he shifted forward to the edge of his chair. "How do you know that?"

"Well, they didn't say your name, but they spoke of a servant boy seeing the jester doing some kind of magic."

"So that *is* what he was doing in that room. He was speaking so strangely. I couldn't understand him at all."

"So you did see him? What was all of that talk about a gem and a skull?"

Jacob proceeded to tell Catherine about his encounter with the jester that morning. He even described the intense longing and desire to run toward the skull and try to pick it up.

"Well, you wouldn't have been able to pick it up," Catherine said when he was finished. "I heard them talk about how heavy it is and how they couldn't get the gem out with a hammer, a sword, or by magic. The jester must have been speaking Latin. I don't know much about magic, but I think that most magical spells are written in Latin. I do know a few words such as, arbor, cibus, and equus, but I never really liked it very much, so Elizabeth said we could stop the lessons."

"Well, I don't know what language it was, but if it *was* a magical spell, it surely wasn't working. I do know that I intend to get into that room for a better look," Jacob said. He fell back into the soft, pillowy chair and rested his chin on top of his interlocked fingers.

Jacob and Catherine sat there quietly for a minute or two.

After a while Jacob yawned and said, "It is getting late now, but we have some planning to do over the next few days. Let's try to talk some more tomorrow evening. I want to tell you about my trip to the woods." Remembering his promise to Raoul, he quickly added, "Not too much happened, but I did nearly get lost in the forest."

"Sounds very exciting, my young adventurer," Catherine replied sarcastically. "I can't wait to hear all about the trees."

A short time later, as Jacob lay in bed trying to fall asleep, he thought back again on all that had happened that day. For as long as he could remember, nothing exciting or unusual had ever happened in his life. *Today was sure different*, he thought.

Eventually, he fell asleep and had dreams of magic and forests and secret rooms. At one point he dreamt that a white skull with a deep blue gem in its forehead called out to him, but just as he was about to touch it, he woke suddenly.

After quickly sitting up in bed, Jacob held his breath and listened carefully, wondering if the skull had actually called his name, but his room was dark and quiet. He rested his head on the pillow again, and just as before, sleep was fleeting.

CHAPTER 10

Jacob awoke the next morning without feeling refreshed. "This is going to be a long day," he mumbled as he swung his legs around and stumbled out of bed.

The servants' rooms were quite small, so just a small step later he was standing in front of his garment coffer. His weariness made him grateful for his cramped quarters that particular morning.

After getting dressed and making himself presentable, Jacob headed down to the main floor and wandered toward the kitchen. He took a circuitous route, passing by all the possible locations that might allow for a happenstance meeting with Catherine. A few minutes later, disappointed, Jacob stepped into the kitchen. The aroma of broiled mutton, freshly baked bread, and roasted apples lifted his spirits.

Even though the castle servants and king's guards were not allowed to eat until King Humphrey and Queen Millicent had finished their meals, there was plenty of food to go around. The heavy taxes imposed by the current monarchy could be paid with gold or with other commodities such as livestock, grain, or fruit. As such, food in the castle was plentiful, and the cooks made sure to prepare enough for both the royal appetites and for the numerous servants and guards.

"Good morning, Master Jacob!" bellowed William, one of the cooks, upon seeing Jacob come through the kitchen doorway. William was a short, stout man, who was always loud and in a good mood. His round, red face, had big, bright eyes and a perpetual wide grin that made his mood contagious. He had started calling Jacob master as a joke when Jacob was a young child and had continued the greeting over the years.

"Fetch me my breakfast instantly!" ordered Jacob as he stuck out his chest and tried his best to sound like King Humphrey.

"You've gone from master to king, I see." William laughed and handed a plate of steaming food across the counter that separated the cooking space from the dining area of the kitchen.

"Alas, William, I am but a humble servant…and a hungry one at that." Jacob sat at the nearest table and began shoveling the tender mutton into his mouth.

"I'm not sure about the humility, but I can see that the hunger is sincere."

Jacob turned around and jumped to his feet. Smiling widely, he said, "Good morning, Catherine. Would you care to join me? My servant, William, will gladly bring you some food." Jacob waited for the princess to take a seat across from him before sitting down again.

"It would be my honor to serve the princess," replied the smiling chef as he came around the counter and placed a plate of food in front of Catherine.

"Thank you, William. You are a master chef and a kind man."

William beamed with pride and for once in his life was speechless as he walked back around to the other side of the countertop and began cooking again. Jacob and Catherine ate their food intently and spoke occasionally about nothing in particular. They had been friends for so long that they were comfortable with an occasional silence and never felt the need to force a conversation.

Before long, many of the servants and guards had filtered through the kitchen's service entrance, and the room was full of people eating and talking loudly with one another. The servants were a close-knit group—much like a family. Jacob looked around the room at their kind faces and smiled—he knew them all very well.

The guards, however, were different. They always gravitated toward the same section of tables in the corner of the kitchen and mostly kept to themselves. Other than Ossian and one or two others, they were not very friendly to Jacob or the other servants.

For the most part they were rough men who seemed to enjoy enforcing the tyrannical laws of the king.

Jacob glanced over his shoulder and saw the captain of the royal guards, Ambrose, speaking to the others. The captain spent the majority of his days traveling throughout the kingdom, enforcing the laws and collecting taxes. He and his men would return periodically with the money and goods that they had collected and present them to the king. Quite often they would have in tow a peasant or two to add to the crowded prison cells .

King Humphrey would quickly listen to the pleas of his new prisoners, pronounce their guilt, and send them directly to the dungeons. Ambrose would stay for a day or two and then begin his legal plundering again. Jacob was intimidated by Ambrose and was glad that he was only around on rare occasions.

Leaning closer to Catherine so that he could be heard above the clamor, Jacob joked, "If I don't get some breakfast up to the jester soon, he might try some of that powerful magic on me."

"I'm coming along this time," Catherine insisted. "Last time I missed way too much excitement. I don't think it's a good idea to take the jester and his magic too lightly. He seemed like a possessed man when he was talking to my father yesterday, and I have always thought there was something sinister and dangerous about him."

"You might be right. I don't know much about magic, and I am guessing that he doesn't either, but I don't want to find out the hard way that I'm wrong."

Jacob and Catherine stood up and weaved their way through the crowded kitchen to the counter.

"William, prepare a plate for the jester or I shall have Ambrose throw you into the dungeon," Jacob demanded.

"Even Ambrose obeys your word now, does he? I had better hurry then, master," replied William as he spooned some breakfast onto a tray and smiled.

"This is becoming tiresome." The princess rolled her eyes in feigned disgust.

CHAPTER 11

After passing by the royal quarters, Jacob and the princess turned right at the hallway that led to the southwest spiral staircase.

"Why are we going this way, Catherine? It would have been faster to go past the royal dining room to the other stairwell."

"That's the most likely area to run into my parents, and I don't want to sit down for another breakfast right now."

As they passed by the drawing room and approached the princess's quarters, they heard a faint whistle coming from their left. They were surprised to see the door to the princess's room slightly ajar and a hand motioning them to enter.

Jacob instinctively stepped in front of the princess, putting himself between her and the door. "Who's there?"

The door opened slightly wider, and a well-known face materialized briefly before disappearing again into the darkness of the room. It was the kind face of Blythe, the queen's seamstress. She was nearly sixty-five years old, and the evidence of the years of toil in the service of the queen had become obvious in her white hair and wrinkled features.

Catherine, upon seeing that it was Blythe, quickly stepped around Jacob, grabbed his hand, and pulled him into the room. Blythe hastily shut the door behind them and turned the deadbolt.

"What's this about, Blythe?" the princess asked. "You nearly scared the life right out of me."

"I'm sorry, Princess Catherine, but I would like to talk to you in private."

"Yes, of course," said Jacob as he stepped toward the door, still holding the tray of food. "I'll deliver the jester his breakfast, and we can talk later, Catherine."

"Thank you. I will look for you at dinner then," the princess replied.

Back inside the room, Catherine noticed a worried look on the face of the seamstress. "Blythe, what is it that you want to talk about? You seem worried."

"I've been keeping a secret for seventeen years, more or less. I was sworn to secrecy by the king and queen under penalty of death if I should ever divulge it. I have exceeded my allotted number of years in this life, and I'm weary." She sat into a comfortable chair near the door, shoulders slumped, and sighed.

The princess had mixed emotions. She felt as if she was about to get some answers to the questions she had long held in her heart, yet she knew that she would be asking a lot if she urged the seamstress to continue.

"Blythe, you are a dear friend and have always been kind to me. I don't want to see you this way. Please forgive me for putting you in this situation and go back to your duties."

"Catherine, I have made up my mind, and I intend to go on. Please listen carefully as I will not be able to tell you a second time."

"I understand," replied the princess as she pulled a chair closer to the tired seamstress and sat directly across from her.

Blythe raised her eyes to Catherine's and began her story. "Many years ago I lived with my husband and young son in a cottage not far from the small town of Woodhurst. My husband was a farmer and raised a few sheep and cattle to provide for our family. My mother taught me the art of sewing at a young age, and I was skilled at making clothing and linens. I would often travel to Strathwick with a group of peasants from Woodhurst to sell our goods in the large markets. One day after returning from the journey, I arrived home to find both my husband and my son very ill. I treated them with herbs and balms for nearly three days straight. My little son passed on the fourth day—my husband joined him soon after."

Catherine sat quietly as the seamstress paused from her story. She waited for Blythe to continue. "I buried them myself in a hole that I dug under my son's favorite tree. Then, after gathering all of the valuables that I could take with me, I herded the animals to Woodhurst and sold them. I traveled to Strathwick, rented a room, and began sewing. I sewed my sorrow away for weeks and weeks. When I was finished and my heart was healed ever so slightly, I had a collection of the finest gowns, linens, and tunics that I had ever made. As I sold them in the markets, word quickly spread about my fine clothing and uncommon sewing talents. It wasn't long before an esquire on errand from King Rowland and Queen Mary knocked on my door and escorted me to the castle in which we now sit."

"So that's how you became the royal seamstress," Catherine reasoned. She was fascinated by the story and glad to know of Blythe's history, but she still couldn't figure out what deep secret was about to be revealed.

"I happily served the previous monarchy for eight years before the king died of his sudden illness. The queen, distraught and alone, must have done as I did and left the reminders of her husband behind to start a new life. I've never seen her since."

"So soon after the funeral my parents arrived at the castle?"

"When Humphrey and Millicent arrived things changed. The servants were not permitted to address the king and queen without first being spoken to. We were not allowed into certain rooms in the castle without being summoned, and we were expected to be absolutely invisible when guests were present.

"The castle was no longer a happy and pleasant place to be, and it seemed to me that the king and queen themselves were searching for something to make them content. Humphrey sought after gold and silver and other fine goods in an effort to be happy. Millicent turned to food and sleep and expensive clothing. I was required to make gowns and capes and undergarments from the most exquisite silks and fabrics that could be found. Nothing seemed to satisfy her."

"I know that she can be difficult to live with and often short tempered," Catherine admitted, "but she seems more content now than you describe."

"One day things improved slightly," Blythe said, hesitating to go on.

Catherine waited.

"The king and queen called all of the servants together into the throne room. After everyone had arrived, the queen addressed us boldly. She had a slight glimmer in her eyes as she spoke.

"'As you are all likely aware,' she said, 'The king and I have been unable to have children of our own. This has been a difficult thing for us. However, we would like to announce that we have some very good news—my brother's wife has died during childbirth! Better yet, we have just returned from Dalcaster and have adopted his new daughter as our own. She shall be known as Catherine and is the royal princess of Avondale.'"

Catherine was stunned. A thousand thoughts raced through her head. She felt sadness and anger, relief and peace, all at the same time. After a minute or two of silence she simply said, "Thank you for telling me. I won't say a thing to anyone about this until the time is right. Even then your name shall be left out of it—you have my word."

"Thank you, Princess Catherine," replied Blythe.

It seemed to Catherine that she had put a special emphasis on the word *princess*.

The seamstress had a look of relief in her eyes as she went on to explain that each servant had been threatened to never reveal to the princess or any other person that Catherine was not the true daughter of the king and queen. "It bothered me for years not to be able to tell you the truth. Now I wish I would have said something sooner."

"Never mind that," Catherine replied. "The timing is right. I have some thinking to do now—if you will excuse me."

Blythe stood, embraced the princess, and left the room.

After the door closed quietly, Catherine went to her bed, lay down, and wept. Even she didn't know what the tears represented—she just needed to cry.

CHAPTER 12

Jacob was disappointed as he started back down the long set of straight stairs. When he had arrived at the top floor with the jester's lukewarm breakfast the mysterious room was locked up tight. He knocked on the jester's door and was simply told to set the plate of food down and be gone. For as long as Jacob could remember he had walked up those stairs, dropped off the food, and returned to the servant's floor without a single suggestion of excitement. Yesterday was an exception, and he worried that his mundane servitude had returned.

As he descended the staircase, Jacob thought of the mysterious skull, his wanderings in the forest, his encounter with Raoul, the peasant travelers, and the woman rider on the jet-black horse. He even wished, briefly, for the excitement that he had felt while sneaking back into the castle grounds, knowing that if he was caught he would be severely punished. Yesterday had stirred his soul. A seed was planted. He wanted excitement and adventure. Yesterday had been a day to remember. "Today will be a day to forget," he said grumpily as he reached the bottom step.

Knowing that Ambrose and his men were back in the castle for a couple of days, Jacob quickly finished his inside chores and hurried to the stables. The extra horses that needed to be cared for whenever the royal ruffians returned for their brief stay required most of Jacob's time.

He spent the next few hours working vigorously. He mucked out all of the two dozen stalls and spread out a thick layer of fresh pine bedding over the floors. He rinsed and refilled each of the large water buckets and supplied each stall with fresh fodder for the horses. He also brushed each horse thoroughly, starting at the head and working toward the hindquarters. He combed the horses' manes and tails and picked out mud and dirt from their hooves.

When he was through with the horses, he oiled all of the saddles, reins, and bridles to keep them supple and polished. All of this effort was necessary because Jacob never knew when the king was going to walk in unannounced and demand an inspection. If a single item was not to his royal liking, King Humphrey would command Jacob to start all over and do it again— even if it meant removing the clean shavings that had just barely been spread around.

Jacob didn't mind his time in the stables, even if it did leave him sweaty, tired, and quite smelly. The hard work was good for his body and mind. As dinnertime arrived Jacob stood at the door of the main stable, crossed his arms, and proudly looked at the results of his labors. As he stood there admiring the cleanliness of the floors and stalls, the shiny, smooth coats of the horses, and the neatly organized saddles and reins, Jacob realized that the royal horses were treated with more kindness and respect than the castle servants. Looking down at his own ragged clothing and filthy hands, Jacob said, "If I had a servant to care for me as well as I do for the horses, I might look a little more presentable."

Remembering that he had one more thing to do, Jacob retrieved the oil that he had used for the horses' saddles and ran slowly through the gardens to the main gate. Ossian was on his usual watch and saw Jacob approach.

"It seems all was well with your tardiness last evening."

"Yes, I was lucky. Thank you for looking out for me."

"You're a good young man, Jacob, and I didn't want to see you unjustly punished." Changing the subject, he added, "I see that you have some oil for the hinges. Do you plan on another late return any time soon?"

"You never can be too careful. Besides, I have tasted excitement and can't be held accountable for my future actions." Jacob walked over and oiled the old rusty hinges.

"Or don't *want* to be held accountable," Ossian said with a smile.

Checking for possible squeaks, Ossian slowly swung the heavy gate as far as it could open and then back again. As the gate latched with a slight click, the two friends looked at each other and grinned widely.

"I would bet those hinges haven't been oiled for many years." Ossian laughed. "To think that I have listened to those screeches and squeaks for no good reason all this time."

"I know that *I* haven't oiled them before today, and no one else does any real work around here," Jacob joked as he went over and applied a little more oil just in case. "Well, Ossian, I am off to bathe before I offend someone else with my stench. Besides, I've worked up an appetite and I'm afraid the food may be put away soon."

"I've already eaten, and it is a good thing too since that horsey odor of yours would have definitely affected my desire for food." Jacob laughed and walked toward the castle, careful to stay directly upwind of Ossian. He wanted to get even for that last remark.

It wasn't long before Jacob was bathed, dressed in clean clothes, and sitting in the kitchen eating his dinner. King Humphrey and Queen Millicent ate their dinner at exactly one o'clock every afternoon. The servants and guards came to the kitchen whenever they could take a break from their daily chores and duties. There was usually food available between half past one o'clock and three o'clock.

Jacob had arrived later than usual and sat there eating all alone and feeling a bit sorry for himself. He had really hoped that Catherine would come and visit while he was caring for the horses. He was curious about her strange encounter with Blythe and had expected her to come and discuss it with him. She never did.

Finished with his meal, Jacob placed his empty plate on the kitchen counter and left for the royal quarters. The slothful monarchs could usually be found lying around in their chambers, lazily digesting their most recent feast. Every afternoon after dinner Jacob was expected to check in with the queen to receive any additional assignments or chores.

It seemed to Jacob that Queen Millicent would then deliberately assign the most terrible jobs she could possibly imagine. Jacob disliked these afternoon jobs as much as the dreaded chamber pot that he emptied each morning. Just a few days earlier, Jacob was actually told to go into the queen's closet, smell the inside of each of her shoes, and throw away the ones that were particularly offensive. The queen had a lot of shoes. Most were offensive.

Jacob approached the door timidly, gave his usual knock of three soft taps, and heard the queen yell rudely, "Who is it, and what do you want?"

Surprised that the queen still hadn't figured out the daily routine after all of these years, Jacob replied, "It's just Jacob, Your Highness. Do you have a chore for me this afternoon?"

"Yes! Go and check the dungeons for dead prisoners. I thought I smelled something foul earlier this morning."

"Yes, Your Highness," Jacob replied loudly through the door. "Although it is probably just your own feet," he added, too quietly to be heard.

Jacob had never been down to the prison cells. He had heard it was a dreadful place. It was rumored that even without the smell of dead prisoners the abundance of sewage, rotting food scraps, and un-bathed bodies created an awful stench. It was no wonder that the guards always stayed on the stairwell side of the thick, locked door.

As he approached the unfamiliar guards Jacob said, "Excuse me, sirs, the queen has asked me to make a quick inspection of the prisoners."

Without uttering a single word, one of the guards got up from his chair, unlatched at least a dozen strong locks, and opened the door just wide enough for Jacob to slip through. The stink hit Jacob like a battering ram. Lifting up his shirt to his nose, Jacob slid through the doorway apprehensively. The heavy door slammed shut behind him, locks clicking away.

Jacob swallowed hard. To his left he saw a large wooden barrel full of dingy, grimy water. "That must be the drinking water—I might prefer death by thirst," he muttered.

There were twenty-seven prison cells in this gloomy dungeon, but most of them had more than one prisoner trapped within. It was laid out in a rectangular shape with nineteen of the cells around the perimeter and the other eight cells in the center. Jacob's plan was to make only one pass around the hallway, glancing back and forth from his right to his left constantly and surveying each cell quickly. With any luck he would soon be walking back up the spiral staircase to the main floor.

Hopefully the guards will open the door for me when I am done, Jacob thought. *Maybe this is a clever way of punishing me because of yesterday.*

The prisoners had all stood up, their chains clanking loudly, and approached the bars facing the hallway when they heard the door hinges creak.

As Jacob started down the ill-lit hallway, he heard prisoners calling out for help from all directions. Many of them reached their thin, cadaverous arms through the bars in an effort to grab him and get his attention. At times, Jacob pulled away from one grasp just to be seized by another hand from the opposite side of the narrow corridor. The many pale-white faces were gaunt and scraggy with deep-set eyes and wide, black pupils. Long matted beards, rotting brown teeth, and torn, ragged clothing stood as proof that most of them had been locked up for many years.

As he made his second left turn and was nearly halfway done with his inspection, Jacob's shirt was seized from behind, and he was jerked backward into the solid steel bars. Surprisingly strong hands wrenched his arms behind him and wrapped around his wrists with a vice-like grip. Struggling to free himself, Jacob writhed and twisted until it felt like his arms would snap.

After realizing that he was unable to free himself, he gave up his fight and yelled, "What do you want from me? I have no keys, food, or even dirty water. I can no more free you from this wretched place than turn the iron bars into gold!"

The voice that whispered into Jacob's ear was quiet and surprisingly feeble considering the strength of the prisoner's grip. The haunting voice struggled to get the words out as it slowly said, "Youv' come beck from th' utha world, I see? Hev' you finushed yur sleep? Why d'you com to botha' me here, knowin' thet I'd soon join you. Or paheps I 'ready hev… Yes, I b'leev thet is th' case."

The feeble voice trailed off as the prisoner's grip loosened. Realizing that this was his opportunity to escape, Jacob lurched forward while twisting his body. A second later he had freed himself. Then, when he spun around to see who had held him, Jacob beheld a tall, wiry man, with a very long beard, squatting down and rocking back and forth.

This ghost-like figure was picking at the stone floor with his finger and rambling softly. He acted as if Jacob was not even there. Jacob noticed a long, deep groove in the stone where the prisoner was picking. It had been worn down significantly over the years, and even in the dim light Jacob could see that the man's finger was calloused and hard.

This man has been trapped down here for so long that he has lost his mind, Jacob thought as he slowly turned and started back down the corridor, careful to stay as far away from the cells as possible.

It seemed to Jacob like an eternity passed by, but a few minutes later he finished his cell check and quickly knocked on the thick prison door. He hadn't seen any dead prisoners, but there were plenty who seemed just a moment away from that fate. Jacob wondered if death would be a welcome relief to many of them.

Jacob knocked again, and after another agonizing period of time he heard the numerous locks turn and saw the door open. Quickly stepping through the door, he took a giant breath of almost-fresh air. The two disheveled guards were smiling noticeably, and Jacob realized that they had intentionally delayed opening the door in order to give him a fright. It had worked.

"Did you enjoy your time in there?" joked one of the guards. "Now you know why we sit out here."

"That was far from enjoyable. That poor prisoner in the corner grabbed me and said some strange things that I didn't even understand. Then all of a sudden he acted as if it never happened and started rubbing the floor with his finger."

"That's Crazy Cuthbert, but he hasn't spoken a word in ages. Rumor has it that he was a very successful thief in his time. Every time the previous king let him out he would start stealing again. Eventually it was decided he would have to stay here permanently. It's been nearly thirty years, and he may be one of the few prisoners who truly deserves this place."

Not wanting to linger near the prison cells, Jacob hurried up the stairs to report to the queen. He decided as he approached the door to the royal quarters that he would gladly smell her shoes whenever he was asked if it meant that he wouldn't have to enter the dungeon again.

I would even smell them with her feet still in them, Jacob thought as the ghostly faces of the prisoners flashed through his mind.

CHAPTER 13

When Jacob awoke the next morning he felt even more tired than he had the day before. After reporting to the queen that all of the prisoners were still living at the time he finished his inspection—but possibly not for much longer—she proceeded to give him a long list of odd jobs and general castle repairs to complete. He spent the rest of the afternoon and evening following her orders.

Jacob was so alarmed by his visit to the dungeon that he even skipped supper and worked late into the night in order to complete his list of chores. He was now truly afraid of the consequences of not obeying the royal couple's every command. To make matters worse, not only was he physically fatigued, but he had once again suffered through a restless night's sleep.

Jacob rushed through his morning routine; he was famished. When he arrived at the bustling kitchen, he found Catherine already sitting at her usual table.

"Two days in a row without having to eat breakfast in the dining room?" Jacob asked as he sat across from the princess.

William brought him a heaping plate of food as if he could sense Jacob's hunger and quickly went back to cooking.

"I'm going for the all-time record of five days straight."

"I didn't get to see you after our strange encounter with Blythe." Seeing the smile fade from the princess's face, he quickly added, "I had to inspect the dungeons yesterday. I hope I never have to do that again."

"You went into the dungeons?" questioned the princess so loudly that most of the people in the kitchen turned and looked. "What was it like?" she added more quietly as she leaned forward.

"It was frightening and sickening, and I won't soon forget it, although I would like to."

The two friends ate their food without speaking any further.

When they were finished Jacob stood up to get a plate for the jester. "Well, I am off to deliver another breakfast. It's strange that the jester is too good to eat in the kitchen but not good enough to eat with your parents. He must get lonely dining alone."

"I've never seen him eat, yet you only deliver his morning meal. I wonder where and when he eats dinner and supper."

"I sure don't know. Maybe he conjures them up out of mid air," Jacob said with a laugh.

"Well, I'm coming with you today since I wasn't able to yesterday morning. I need some excitement too."

"As you wish, Your Highness," replied Jacob with a bow, pleased that Catherine was coming along.

Jacob and Catherine picked up the jester's tray and left the busy kitchen, walking toward the southwest staircase. Passing by Catherine's room—this time without interruption—they went up the spiral steps to the servants' and guards' floor. As they turned the corner and headed toward the straight staircase, Jacob stopped suddenly and grabbed the princess's forearm.

"What is it?" Catherine asked as she jumped sideways. "You startled me."

"I just remembered where I have seen that coat of arms before!"

"What are you talking about? What coat of arms?" asked the very confused princess.

"It was in the secret room the other day. As I was quickly glancing around the room before I saw the skull, I saw a large collection of old objects and artifacts. Many of the tapestries, shields, and other items had a crest or something on them. It was also on Raoul's sword."

"Raoul? Who's Raoul?"

"I'll tell you later. Come on. We are getting into that room." Jacob rushed down the hallway toward the stairs.

"Slow down or you'll spill the jester's breakfast again. Besides, how are we going to get in without the key?" yelled the princess as she tried to keep up.

When she reached the bottom of the stairs Catherine looked up and saw that Jacob was climbing the stairs three steps at a time. Before she was halfway up the long flight of stairs he had disappeared completely. Hurrying as quickly as she could, she soon arrived at the top step. Her heart was pounding, her side ached, and she was completely winded.

While bending over to catch her breath, the princess turned her head and looked down the long hallway. Jacob was standing in front of the closed door with the tray of food sitting on the ground next to him. He turned and looked at Catherine, and with one hand motioned for her to come forward. With his other hand he held his finger to his lips.

Catherine inched forward step by step, her heart now pounding from excitement rather than fatigue. When she was still a few steps away from Jacob, he pointed at the door excitedly. He had a wide grin on his face. Soon Catherine was standing next to Jacob and saw that not only was the door unlocked, it was slightly open.

"How did you get the door open?" she whispered to Jacob.

"It was like this when I got here."

"The jester must be inside, or he wouldn't have left the door like that. We should knock just in case," Catherine said nervously.

"Then he might hear us from his bedroom—if he is still in there. Besides, I've been standing here quietly now for some time, and I haven't heard any noises coming from inside. I say we go in."

"Well, let's do it quickly then. The longer we stand out here in the hallway, the more likely we are to be seen."

Jacob eased the door open very slowly, hoping that it wouldn't make a noise. When it was open just wide enough to slide through, he slipped in and reached back for Catherine. She grabbed his hand and followed him in quietly. Jacob then pushed the door until it was nearly closed, leaving it just as they had found it.

Catherine hadn't been in the room before, and after first scanning quickly for any sign of the jester, she started looking around more intently. She loved old heirlooms and was thrilled to see a room packed full of them. She saw furniture of the finest craftsmanship, beautiful paintings and statues, exquisite pottery, tapestries, and many silver and pewter dishes and candlesticks. She even admired the shiny armor, shields, and swords that were scattered throughout the room. Nothing seemed to have been broken or ruined in any way, but it definitely wasn't organized at all.

The chaotic mess made the room even more intriguing to Catherine as she imagined what wonderful artifact might be hiding just behind the ones that she could see. She wanted to start moving things and searching for more treasures of the past but knew there wasn't time. Besides that, they couldn't make a single sound if they wanted to avoid being caught.

Remembering what Jacob had said about the crest, Catherine stepped toward a large, silk banner hanging on the wall closest to her. She wanted to examine it more closely. Some of the lower part of the banner was covered by a chest of drawers, but Catherine could still see the coat of arms in its center. It was definitely different from the one that represented her adoptive parents' monarchy.

In the center of the crest Catherine saw a large, elaborate shield with its face divided into four quarters. The quarters bore the figures of a crown, a wolf, a fish, and a sword. Supporting the left side of the shield was a golden lion with its front paws raised up so that they were touching the side of the shield. On the right side was a sizable and powerful brown bear. It too was standing on its hind legs and resting its forepaws on the shield's side. A large hawk was grasping the top of the shield with its sharp talons. Its powerful wings were spread wide. Beneath it all was a waving banner with the word, "AVONDALE," written in large, capital letters. It was a work of art.

"This must be the coat of arms representing King Rowland's monarchy," she whispered excitedly as she turned to look at Jacob. "All of these wonderful things must have been moved here after my parents inherited the kingdom."

Jacob didn't even turn to look at her.

"Jacob, did you hear me?" she asked, speaking a little louder this time.

Jacob just stood there with his eyes fixed in the other direction. The princess realized that she had been so excited about the treasures packed into the other side of the room that she had totally forgotten about the real reason they had snuck in.

After quickly walking over to where Jacob was standing, she saw the strange white skull with the deep blue gem set into its forehead. It was interesting and a little frightening as it sat there all alone on the shelf, yet she was more interested in discussing the coat of arms and the man named Raoul that Jacob had mentioned, so she leaned closer and asked again, "Did you hear me, Jacob?"

Jacob's body remained completely still. Without even turning to look at Catherine, he said, "Can you hear it?"

"Hear what?"

"It's calling out to me," he answered with a far-off voice.

"Jacob, you're frightening me," she said as she touched his arm. "Have you been staring like that since we came into the room?"

"It wants me to pick it up," he said, not even answering her question.

"I don't hear a thing, but we need to leave. It can't be moved anyway. Don't you remember what the jester and my father said? Let's get out of here."

"No!" yelled Jacob as he rushed to the shelf and grabbed the skull. It lifted off of the shelf easily, and Jacob turned around and faced the princess, raised the skull high over his head with both hands, and threw it hard to the ground.

A thunderous crash rang through the room, much louder than it should have been. The princess turned her head and put her hands over her ears to soften the deafening noise. After a few moments, frightened and bewildered, Catherine looked back toward Jacob and saw him standing over a pile of fragmented bones at his feet.

Jacob raised his eyes, looked at her, and asked, "What happened?"

"I don't know why, but you were in some kind of a trance. You weren't yourself."

The door directly behind Catherine suddenly swung open, and the jester stepped in quickly. He seemed nearly maniacal as he slammed the door behind him and smirked conspicuously.

"I knew it!" he said. "When I saw the way you were looking at that skull the other day, I knew it had some kind of power over you."

"You *wanted* me to come in here?" Jacob asked with a puzzled look on his face.

"I had a feeling that you would find a way to get that priceless gem freed from that wretched skull. But even if you didn't, I knew that when you came out I could turn you over to the king and tell him of your insubordination. Now it is even better—I get the gem, and you still get the consequences. Now give it to me this instant."

"What would I want with a gem that valuable anyway?" asked Jacob. "There's no way I could sell it. It might as well be a worthless stone from the Stanbourne River." He reached down and picked up the flawless gem from next to the pile of bones and held it out in front of him.

The jester rushed forward, jealous that Jacob was holding the priceless stone, and quickly took it from him. However, as soon as he seized the gem with his right hand there was a flash of bright light. Screaming out in pure agony, the jester dropped the gem to the floor and pulled his right hand into his tunic to cover it up and try to stop the pain.

With his hand throbbing and his eyes wide with anger, he looked up at Jacob and yelled, "What have you done to me, servant boy? You will pay for this!" The jester looked back down and began to unwrap his injured hand.

Jacob and Catherine watched as the little man slowly removed his hand from his tunic, afraid of what he might see but wanting to survey the damage. Catherine cringed noticeably as she saw that his thumb and three of his fingers had been so gravely injured that all that remained were four charred stumps extending slightly past the palm of the hand. His index finger was also burnt badly enough that the tip was missing down to the top knuckle, just below where the fingernail should have been. His palm was severely charred and blistered.

Upon seeing the devastation to his hand and blinded with pain and anger, the jester turned and ran from the room yelling, "Guards! Detain the servant boy and throw him into the dungeon!" Jacob and the princess could hear his voice echoing through the halls as he ran down the stairs and headed toward the main floor. The words, "He's upstairs! Arrest him! Don't let him get away!" reverberated throughout the castle.

"Catherine, I must run. I won't be held prisoner in that horrible place."

"Hurry then. You should try and leave through the kitchen's service entrance. Run to the stables and get a horse. I'll try and stall the guards and meet you there." She quickly ran from the room.

Without thinking, Jacob bent down and picked up the priceless gem that the jester had dropped just moments before. As he did so, he saw out of the corner of his eye that there was still something lying beneath the pile of white, bony shards located a few inches away. Quickly brushing away some of the fragments, Jacob found a small silk pouch that was the exact same color as the gem itself.

"That must have been hidden inside the skull," he whispered as he reached over and picked it up. Jacob quickly opened the pouch and dropped the precious, oval gem inside. As the gem settled into the bottom of the pouch, Jacob thought he heard a very slight clinking sound.

Wanting to investigate further but knowing that the guards would soon arrive, Jacob swiftly closed the silk pouch tight with its long drawstring, making a nice long loop. He then pulled the loop over his head, placed the pouch around his neck, and tucked it beneath his shirt. After glancing back at the fragmented skull one last time, Jacob dashed from the room.

CHAPTER 14

There were many questions racing through Jacob's mind as he descended the long staircase toward the servants' floor. *Why can I touch the gemstone but the jester can't? Which hallway should I run down to avoid being caught? Will I ever see Catherine again? Why didn't the skull affect her like it did me? If the jester has magic, why didn't he try and use it to capture me? How will I get out of the castle grounds?*

Jacob had no answers to any of these questions, but he did know that he needed to run. In fact, he felt a surge of energy enter his body, and it seemed to him that he was running faster than he had ever run before. After reaching the bottom landing in five long strides, Jacob sped toward the northwest staircase. Sooner than he thought possible, he was turning right and descending the stone steps four at a time.

Catherine must have delayed the guards somehow, Jacob thought.

Seconds later he heard shouting coming from above. "He's gone this way! You three follow, while we block the other stairwell."

Knowing that he couldn't turn back now, Jacob continued down the spiral steps, hearing footsteps echoing from behind.

Just moments later he was at the main floor. As he exited the stairwell, he paused briefly to plan his next move. Straight up ahead were five guards blocking his way to the kitchen. To his right he saw at least a dozen guards standing shoulder to shoulder, preventing him from exiting through the main castle doors. To make matters worse, within seconds the three guards who had followed him down the staircase would soon overtake him from behind.

"Halt!" cried out one of the guards from his right.

Jacob turned and looked directly at him. Stepping forward from the line of guards and holding his sword in front of him was Ambrose, captain of the royal guards.

After a slight pause he yelled, "Seize him!"

The guards let out a cry and rushed at him from all sides. Remembering how the dungeons had treated Crazy Cuthbert and all of the other ghostly prisoners, Jacob chose to run.

He raced down the hallway with astounding speed. He was running for his life. Gasping for air, he leapt through the dining room door—the guards hot on his trail.

Sitting at the dining room table was Queen Millicent, eating a post-breakfast snack.

"Jacob, what on earth are you doing? You aren't allowed in this room!"

"I really must be going."

The queen gasped. Ambrose and his men charged through the door just behind Jacob. Six more guards rushed through the narrow door at the other end of the room. They drew their swords and ran toward Jacob—three on each side of the long table.

Jacob instinctively took two long strides toward the queen and leapt up onto the table directly in front of her. His feet scattered plates, glasses, and bowls everywhere, covering the queen from head to toe with food. Jacob sprinted across the top of the long table, hurdling candlesticks with ease.

The guards were in pursuit again, but they had failed to recognize Jacob's plan until it was too late. With his swift speed and surprising agility, Jacob was confident that he would escape.

Just as he was nearing the end of the table, Jacob saw the king and the jester step into the room, standing side by side a few feet from the table's end. The king looked furious, and the jester was beside himself with rage, his right hand wrapped in a towel.

"Stop him!" bellowed the king. "He has stolen my treasure and used dark magic against my jester. He must be punished!"

The king's words were still echoing throughout the room when Jacob planted his left foot firmly, just inches from the end of the table, and jumped high into the air, arching over the heads of King Humphrey and the court jester. In one fluid motion Jacob completed a graceful front flip and landed in a squat behind them.

He lunged forward through the kitchen and out into the grounds, heading straight for the stables. Too dazed to be impressed, the king and jester tried to turn in pursuit just as the horde of guards arrived at the narrow doorway that Jacob exited through. Bodies collided into a massive heap with arms and legs sticking out everywhere.

"Get off of me, you worthless slabs of lard!" came the king's muffled command from the bottom of the pile. "Capture him immediately or face my wrath!" he yelled into someone's armpit.

As Jacob approached the stables, wondering how he could possibly take the time to get a horse ready to ride, he saw the princess walking backward out of the main stable door. She was leaning back and pulling hard against something but didn't seem to be making any progress.

Confused, Jacob yelled loudly, "Catherine! What are you doing?"

When she heard Jacob's voice the princess looked over her left shoulder and gave a noticeable sigh of relief. A split second later her expression quickly turned to one of panic, and Jacob heard something whiz past his left ear and thump into the ground next to him. It was an arrow. Guards were shooting at him from the battlements.

Just then Jacob heard what sounded like a dozen bowstrings twang all at once. He covered his head with his arms and veered hard to his right. Seconds later, the wooden shafts all missed to his left, but just barely. Continuing to swerve and move as he ran, Jacob tried to make himself as difficult a target as possible.

Seeing Jacob's new predicament and using all of the strength that she could muster, Catherine gave a final heave, and Jacob was surprised to see a very large, chestnut-brown mare appear from the stable door ahead of him. He was grateful for the princess's resourcefulness, but shocked that she had chosen the queen's own horse as his means of escape. It was a brilliant plan though, he realized, since Ambrose and his men would never be able to over-take him.

Jacob quickly covered the distance between himself and the mare. Without missing a step he sprung into the saddle. He then turned and looked down at the princess sorrowfully, wondering if he would ever see her again.

Catherine looked up at him, but when she tried to force her usual smile, it wouldn't materialize. Jacob made a decision.

"Should I add kidnapping to my list of offenses?" he asked, thrusting his hand down for her to take.

"I don't see why not," she replied happily, smiling more brightly than he had ever seen. "I can't stay here anyway, seeing that I am an accomplice to everything." She reached up and placed her hand in his. Jacob swung her up into the saddle behind him.

Ambrose and the guards had exited the castle and were pur-suing once again. "Cease your fire or you'll injure the princess! Close the gate! To your horses!" Ambrose barked to his men.

Jacob spurred the mare into a fast run. Surprisingly, she read-ily obeyed.

As they sped through the castle gardens toward the iron gate, Jacob shouted back to the princess, "Are you sure you want to come? This may be the last you see of the castle and your parents. I fear we won't be forgiven."

"Yes, Jacob, I am sure," she replied.

The mare seemed to sense the urgency of the situation as she galloped across the grounds. Jacob could see the gate beginning to close up ahead. They were still a good distance away.

"We aren't going to make it!" Jacob shouted back. "It's closing too quickly!"

"We'll make it!"

As the distance shortened with each long stride of the mare's powerful legs, the gate slowed noticeably. Close enough to see what was going on, Jacob saw that the man guarding the gate was his good friend Ossian.

Laughing out loud, Jacob turned his head and said, "I see that you have spoken with Ossian recently. I think we will make it through after all."

Moments later Jacob and Catherine and Queen Millicent's mare rushed through the main gate. The gate was open just wide enough for them to pass through. Jacob smiled widely, and Ossian and Catherine winked at each other.

After slamming the gate closed behind them, Ossian quickly locked it and threw the key over the wall, outside of the castle grounds.

Jacob turned the mare to her right, and they started off toward Aberfield.

CHAPTER 15

The only noise that Jacob and Catherine heard for nearly an hour was the steady thumping of the mare's large hooves on the hard dirt road. Jacob was continually looking over his shoulder for any sign of Captain Ambrose and the other guards, but the princess didn't seem concerned. Even with two riders the queen's horse traveled very quickly and showed no signs of slowing down.

Jacob hadn't tried to start a conversation since escaping the castle—partly because it was difficult to communicate while riding so swiftly, but mostly because he didn't know what to say.

He knew that Catherine had just abandoned her life as the princess of Avondale, and he wondered if she realized what that truly meant. She would have eventually become Queen Catherine, the most respected, wealthy, and important woman in the kingdom. Princes from all the surrounding lands would seek after her hand in marriage, and she would likely have her pick of the most handsome. She would never want for anything; it would be a life of comfort and prosperity.

Catherine, on the other hand, was as excited as she could be. She was glad to be rid of all the lessons and the unrealistic expectations of being a princess. She was also free from her parents' incessant nagging. Best of all, she was on an adventure with Jacob, her oldest and closest friend. In fact, she was reminded of the days when they had played together and created adventure stories just like the one they were now embarking upon.

"Jacob, don't you think we should name the mare?" Catherine finally said. "After all, I sort of just inherited her."

After slowing the mare down to a walk so that they could speak more easily, Jacob replied, "Okay, how about Millie?"

"No, I am growing fond of her. Let's give her a proper name. Something like Mabel or Elinor?"

"How about Stilts or I-Don't-Ever-Get-Tired-No-Matter-How-Long-I-Run?"

"Okay then, it's settled. We have both agreed on Mabel," Catherine replied with a laugh.

"All right, Mabel, would you like some water?" Jacob slowed to a stop and slid down from the saddle. He reached out his hand and helped Catherine down. Grabbing the reins to prevent another runaway, Jacob led Mabel to the river for a drink with Catherine walking right beside him.

"The guards' horses have probably had to rest twice already," Jacob pointed out. "I guess I should know since I am the one who exercised and trained them," he added with a slight smile. "I am a little concerned about hiding our tracks when we enter the forest in a couple of hours. I doubt that Ambrose could track us all the way to Raoul's cottage, but I don't want them even seeing where we enter the woods. I'll be breaking my promise as it is just by taking *you* there."

"You keep speaking of this Raoul person as if I should know him. Who is he, and how do you know we can trust him?" asked the princess.

Jacob proceeded to tell Catherine about his wandering through the forest and his encounter with Raoul. Catherine absolutely loved the story and asked all of the proper questions and gave many remarks at just the right times—comments and questions such as, "You could have been killed!" and "Then what did you do?"

When Jacob saw how interested Catherine was in his narrative, he became even more animated and excited as he spoke.

"How do you suppose he got his sword?" asked Catherine when the story was complete. "The crest you saw was the coat of arms representing King Rowland's monarchy. I'm sure of it. And why has he been hiding in the forest all of these years?"

"I don't have any answers right now since Raoul wouldn't respond to any of my questions last time we met. I hope he will today," Jacob replied. "We'd better hurry. It's nearly noon," he added while looking at the sky.

Once again they mounted the saddle, and Mabel began to run. She too seemed to be enjoying herself.

Captain Ambrose frowned as he knelt there, inspecting the ground carefully. He was surrounded by twenty guards commanded to join him in pursuit of the servant boy and the princess, who they had decided was taken against her will. The guards that remained at the castle were ordered to continue with their usual patrols and responsibilities. Ossian had been thrown into the dungeon for helping Jacob in the escape.

Ambrose stood up and addressed his men boldly. "It seems that they are extending their lead. They have yet to rest their horse, and its stride is as long as when we first left the castle. We won't be able to overtake them with speed. I think it is best for us to travel slowly so that we don't exhaust our horses. The queen's mare has speed and stamina, but the size of her hoof print is a liability. They will not escape us. Mount up!"

CHAPTER 16

Jacob and Catherine rode quietly again for another hour. Jacob was deep in thought the whole time, trying to come up with a way to enter the forest without the guards noticing. He couldn't risk leading them into the forest anywhere near the actual trail for fear that they would spread out, search the woods, and eventually discover the cottage.

Feeling confident that they had greatly outdistanced Ambrose and knowing that he was still a mile or two from his usual resting spot where he would locate the forest trail, Jacob decided to try to hide their tracks.

"Catherine, I think we should ride upriver for the next couple of miles. We need to find a way to lose Ambrose and his men, and at least the mare won't be leaving a visible trail. When we get to where the game trail begins we'll need to find a way to leave the river bed and enter the forest without leaving a sign."

"Nature might help us out with that. I see dark clouds forming up ahead. A good heavy rain would hide Mabel's hoof prints."

"Only if the rain comes after we cross the road and not before. It will require some incredible luck, but it may be our best chance." They continued on the road for another hundred yards or so until Jacob found a section of the river that had a very rocky bank. Catherine slid off the horse and picked up a freshly fallen tree branch from the edge of the forest. She then proceeded to follow behind Mabel, walking backward and brushing away any possible tracks left by the horse or her own shoes.

Jacob was busy carefully steering the mare over the rockiest ground he could find and eventually into the river. When Catherine had finished erasing any evidence of their departure from the road, she looked back and laughed. To her untrained eyes it looked as if the horse and riders had just disappeared into thin air. With Jacob's help she climbed back into the saddle behind him.

It was a slow process walking up the Stanbourne River. The current was mild, and the water not too deep for the most part, but going upstream was difficult. Jacob steered the mare around the deepest sections of water but occasionally got nervous when they had to go through an area where they couldn't see the bottom. Luckily, it was a pleasant spring afternoon, and even with wet clothing they weren't too cold. Up ahead, however, the sky was darkening quickly.

It took much longer than Jacob had expected. He had been nervous that this strategy would allow his pursuers to make up the distance between them. But as luck would have it, they eventually found themselves looking directly at the game trail leading into the forest. The only problem was that there was a short section of riverbank and a dirt road between them and where they needed to be, and Jacob couldn't think of a way to get there without leaving a trail of large, unmistakable hoof prints.

Jacob looked up at the angry sky above him. It could begin raining any moment. A wind had picked up and was blowing lightly from the northwest, the sky was darkening with grayish clouds, and the temperature had dropped slightly.

Not feeling as if he could gamble on a rainstorm that may or may not come, however, Jacob said, "I think our best hope is to try and erase our tracks like we did as we entered the river earlier. Maybe we'll get lucky and they won't notice that the road has been smoothed out by branches."

"It could work since they will have lost our actual trail a few miles back and might not be looking too closely as they rush by. They're probably assuming that we will try and out-distance them and end up as far from the castle as possible," Catherine replied with a hint of worry in her voice.

"Let's get on with it then. We certainly can't just stay here in the river until they arrive." Jacob urged the mare slowly out of the river and onto its bank. Mabel responded readily as if she understood what they were trying to do.

"Doesn't it seem like Mabel has been more pleasant today than usual?" Jacob asked as he carefully steered the tall horse along the hardest and driest dirt he could find.

"Maybe she's as excited as I am to be on a real adventure. But she has been on her best behavior it seems."

"Either she has finally taken a liking to me, or she is acting this way for your sake," Jacob said with a laugh. "I would guess that the latter is true since, as I explained to Raoul, she seems to prefer royalty to servants."

"Well, you're no longer a servant, and I am no longer a princess," Catherine replied. "We are both just regular people now, it seems to me."

Jacob didn't know what to say. He realized that the princess had, in effect, given up her royalty. What he hadn't realized was that he was essentially free, assuming he could escape the guards. He suddenly felt exhilarated.

Just a short thirty yards later as they neared the line of trees, Jacob stopped the horse and leapt down from the saddle. Holding up his hand for Catherine's, he helped her dismount.

"Would you mind wiping away our tracks while I throw some dead leaves over the ground leading into the forest? The soil is softer here, and that might prevent a noticeable hoof print from forming." He broke off a small branch and handed it to Catherine.

After taking the branch, Catherine slowly walked back across the road and over to the river, careful to step in the same tracks that Mabel just made. She was happy to see that for the most part the tracks were on hard, dusty earth and could be easily erased. Near the river's edge, however, Catherine saw that there were a number of deeper prints in the soft earth along the bank. She covered three of them with a few small rocks she found beside the riverbank. Two others she carefully concealed with dead vegetation. After hiding the more obvious tracks, she began the chore of erasing the hoof prints on the dirt road.

Jacob finished his work with the fallen leaves and glanced over to see how Catherine was doing. When he saw her he began to laugh uncontrollably. She was crouched in a very strange position, walking backward and looking over her right shoulder. She placed her right foot in the track behind her and then looked ahead and used the branch to wipe away the track she just vacated. Catherine then looked over her other shoulder, trying to find the next track for her left foot. At this point she nearly lost her balance and fell over. Jacob began laughing even harder.

Catherine laughed as well, realizing how silly she must look, which only made it more difficult to keep her balance. Approximately thirty awkward steps and two or three minutes later, and through laughter that actually brought tears to her eyes, Catherine eventually managed to get back to where Jacob was standing.

Turning around, she punched him softly in the arm and said with a smile, "That's for making fun of me while I was trying my best to keep you alive."

"I deserve it. My cheeks hurt from laughing." Jacob wiped a tear from his eye. "I do appreciate your hard work. I don't see a single recognizable track that Ambrose could—"

A bright flash and a loud boom of thunder interrupted Jacob's sentence. Mabel darted forward into the woods, and Catherine was startled so badly she jumped toward Jacob and grabbed his arm. Just seconds later it began raining so hard that it seemed to Jacob as if they were looking out from behind a waterfall.

The two adventurers watched as they saw the road fill with puddles and realized that all of their hard work had just been made completely unnecessary by the flood forming before them. They were wet from head to toe but felt certain that for the moment they were safe from capture.

Jacob and Catherine turned and walked into the forest, still laughing as they went.

"Men, it seems as if we won't be able to track them after all," Ambrose barked from atop his horse.

He and the other guards were completely drenched from the storm, and it didn't look as if the weather was going to slacken any time soon.

"We'll return to the castle for provisions and a good night's rest. In the morning we journey toward Aberfield. I have no doubt that we will capture the boy within a few days and will likely be rewarded handsomely for returning the princess."

Ambrose and his men turned their horses around and sped back to the castle. Heavy rain and soft, muddy earth impeded their progress slightly, but these were hardened men, and tomorrow they would hunt.

CHAPTER 17

Jacob and Catherine stepped into the small clearing that held Raoul's cottage. It wasn't necessary for Jacob to find and follow the markers carved into the tree trunks along the trail since Mabel was able to lead them straight there. She had done so without hesitating or seeming lost along the way.

The rain had subsided, but both companions were now as wet as they would have been had they fallen head first into the Stanbourne River. They were also chilled, since the air temperature had dropped considerably with the coming of the storm. Jacob looked over at Catherine and saw that her long brown hair was lying flat against her head and cheeks and that she had drops of rain falling from her chin. She was shivering. Catherine smiled at him when their eyes met.

She can look beautiful under any circumstances, Jacob thought. He wanted to tell her so, but he didn't, feeling unsure of himself.

"Well, I guess we should go knock." Jacob turned and started toward the cottage. "Don't be surprised if we are greeted with a sword."

"That won't surprise me at all," Catherine replied as she looked at the secluded dwelling and wondered if anyone else had ever been there. She stayed a few steps behind as she followed Jacob toward the door.

As they passed by the corral on their left, Jacob quickly swung open the wooden gate, and Mabel readily walked through. Two other horses appeared from the small stable in the corner and wandered curiously toward Mabel. One of the horses Jacob recognized as Raoul's, but he was surprised to see the other horse. It was a beautiful jet-black mare.

"I've seen that horse before!" Jacob exclaimed. "A woman was riding it alone at dusk the other night when I was returning to the castle. She must have been Raoul's wife returning from some errand in Strathwick."

"It is a marvelous horse, but I don't see why you are so excited over seeing her."

"It all seems so mysterious and strange. I still don't know how Raoul knew my name the other day and why he wouldn't talk about his wife when I asked." Jacob hurried toward the cottage.

Momentarily forgetting his concern over breaking his promise to Raoul, Jacob arrived at the door quickly. Glancing back at Catherine, who had stopped a few feet away, he smiled and said, "Well, if nothing else we can ask for shelter for the night."

Jacob turned back to the door and moved his hand forward to knock, but before he could make contact with the sturdy wood the door swung open quickly. Raoul slipped through the doorway and closed it softly behind him. Looking angry and slightly worried, the strong man glanced over at Catherine and then back at Jacob. His face formed a scowl.

"What are you doing here, and how could you possibly think that bringing the princess of Avondale here would be a good idea?" Raoul asked in an angry whisper.

"It is a long story, but I think that you will understand my reasoning when you hear the details," Jacob answered. "I wouldn't have come if it wasn't absolutely necessary."

Raoul's expression softened, and he turned to Catherine. "Excuse my rudeness, Your Highness. It's just that I thought Jacob and I had an understanding about the secret nature of our little dwelling here."

"I assure you, sir, Jacob has been worried about that very thing all morning and has taken every necessary precaution to keep your secret. I can also assure you that I will tell no one of this location," Catherine replied. "But, if you don't mind my asking, why is it so important that you remain hidden here among the trees?"

"Ah, yes, I have heard of your curious nature," Raoul responded with a slight smile. "The two of you make quite a pair with all of your questions, I'm sure," he added while turning back to Jacob. "Maybe it is time for some answers, though not all at once."

"Thank you," Jacob replied. "We have much to tell you also."

"Well, this probably won't go over well at all, but you might as well come inside and meet my wife," Raoul suggested. "She doesn't know that you are here yet, but I suppose that now is as good a time as any."

Raoul opened the door widely, stepped inside, and said, "Dear, we have visitors!"

CHAPTER 18

When the royal guards returned back to the castle without the servant boy and the princess, things went very badly. A trumpet announced the imminent arrival of the guards, so King Humphrey, Queen Millicent, and the jester rushed out the main castle doors and were waiting in the courtyard. Ambrose arrived at the head of the group, dismounted his steed, and knelt directly before the king.

"I am sorry, my king, but we have lost them," he announced somberly. "We will find them soon. That is my promise."

Upon hearing the bad news, Queen Millicent burst into tears and began sobbing so loudly that King Humphrey was forced to wait before responding to the captain. The queen turned and started walking slowly back toward the main castle doors, burdened by her physical and emotional heft. The king, jester, and all of the royal guards waited in silence until finally the thick wooden doors closed behind her, muffling her wailing considerably.

King Humphrey, having had some time to calm down, turned back to Ambrose and said, "As you can see, the queen is quite distraught over the princess's abduction. She, I mean *we*, would like her returned to us safely as soon as possible. However, there is also the matter of a very valuable gem that the boy has stolen from me. I will reward you handsomely when it is returned."

"And I suggest that you handle it with care!" added the unusual little jester while unwrapping and holding up his deformed hand for all to see.

The group of hardened men, upon seeing the charred and deformed stump that remained, groaned, many looking away in disgust.

Pleased by their reaction, the jester smiled grimly and added, "You may have a harder time arresting this servant than you would expect. He has some kind of magic within him or he wouldn't have been able to obtain the gem and avoid capture so easily."

Ambrose rose to his feet and addressed the king boldly. "My Liege, I repeat my promise to you. We will find them soon, and both your daughter *and* your gem will be returned to you unscathed." Ambrose bowed again, mounted his horse, and led the guards around the castle's south end toward the stables.

The king and the jester turned and started toward the main castle doors when the king mumbled quietly, "One out of two would be an acceptable outcome."

"Yes, the gem is very valuable indeed," the jester agreed.

CHAPTER 19

Raoul's wife was in the bedroom when she heard her husband open the door and announce that they had visitors. She was so completely surprised that she found herself paused in front of the bedroom mirror checking the state of her hair and wondering who could possibly be standing in her kitchen. Try as she might, she couldn't think of a single person that would come to visit, let alone two or more. She had heard Raoul say *visitors,* hadn't she?

Soon her curiosity was such that she could bear it no longer. While walking across the bedroom into the kitchen, she said excitedly, "Visitors? We haven't had—"

Suddenly stopping mid-sentence, Raoul's wife froze and stared at the two people standing in her entryway. As her gaze met with Catherine's, both women opened their eyes wide with astonishment and exclaimed each other's names simultaneously.

"Elizabeth?"

"Princess Catherine?"

Elizabeth's attention then turned to the young man that she saw beside Catherine, and her eyebrows raised even higher. After turning toward Raoul, she attempted to speak but couldn't utter a single word.

It seemed to Elizabeth that the room was beginning to spin. Her mind went blank, her legs felt weak, and then she fainted—falling hard to the floor.

"Elizabeth!" shouted Raoul as he reached her side in three long strides. Quickly picking her up and holding her in his arms, he looked her over carefully. "She seems to be unharmed," he finally said with a look of relief. "I'll go and lay her down on the bed so she can rest."

"That was Elizabeth, my tutor!" Catherine exclaimed. "I hope she is all right. She is very kind. Why do you suppose she fainted when she saw me? Did she hit her head when she fell? Can you believe that she lives here so deep in the woods?"

Jacob smiled and replied, "She was probably surprised to see you standing in her kitchen. After all, they never even have commoners come by and visit, let alone the royal princess of Avondale."

"Well, that seems to have gone just about as well as expected," Raoul said as he returned from the bedroom and motioned for Jacob and Catherine to sit at the table. "We have many things to discuss, it seems."

"Two of my questions have already been answered," Jacob observed. "I now know who your wife is, and I have also discovered the identity of the mysterious woman that I passed on the road the other day."

"She must've been returning home from the castle!" Catherine said excitedly.

"There will be more answers to come. First you must tell me what you are doing in my kitchen," Raoul stated, looking directly at Jacob.

Jacob and Catherine looked at each other as if trying to decide where to start, and after a long pause Jacob turned back to Raoul and said, "Well, to be honest, I have escaped from the castle, and Catherine has sort of...run away."

"What?" exclaimed Raoul. "Is Captain Ambrose tracking you? You are being chased by the royal guards, and you came to my doorstep?"

"Um...yes," Jacob admitted, hanging his head. "I don't think that they can find us here," he quickly added, hoping to keep Raoul from raising his voice again.

"Well if anyone can follow you here, it is Ambrose, and if he does there will be trouble. He is likely to knock on my door with an axe."

"Are you in some kind of trouble?" asked the princess.

"It's worse than that. If he were to find either myself or my wife it would be disastrous." After what seemed like minutes had passed he finally went on to say, "I guess I might as well tell you that I used to be captain of the royal guards, and Ambrose was one of my men. He was ruthless and mean to almost everyone, but he seemed to hold a special hatred toward me as his captain. It was no secret that he longed for my position and rank."

"So you served my parents as their captain?" Catherine asked with astonishment.

"No, Your Highness. I abandoned my duties the day of King Rowland's funeral, and we have been hiding ever since. Elizabeth has taken every precaution necessary not to be recognized as she taught your lessons each week. Humphrey and Millicent agreed to her request that the lessons were never to be interrupted by anyone for any reason. Also, Elizabeth is always cloaked when she travels to and from the castle. Until now she has been seen by no one but you and your parents." He turned and looked at Jacob thoughtfully as if to say something but decided against it.

"Do you mean that Ambrose would recognize her also? Why would he know your wife's identity?" asked the confused princess.

Raoul paused even longer than before, once again sighing deeply, and said, "I believe he *would* recognize her, as would many of the castle servants. You see, my wife is Queen Mary Elizabeth of Avondale, previous wife of King Rowland and the rightful ruler of this land."

Catherine and Jacob were speechless. They glanced at each other with looks of total surprise and then looked back at Raoul in absolute wonder. Jacob had been hoping all along to learn a few things about Raoul's intense desire for secrecy, but he had no idea that the secret would be of this magnitude. Still, no one spoke for quite some time.

Finally, Jacob said, "So if I understand this correctly, your wife, Queen Mary, the rightful ruler of this kingdom, goes back to the royal castle each week and tutors Princess Catherine while trying to hide her true identity?"

"Twice a week, but yes, you have explained it quite well." Raoul smiled. "Humphrey and Millicent don't know who Elizabeth is either. They never met her before the funeral, and when she was there she was wearing a widow's veil. Besides that, it has been nearly twenty years, and since she hasn't been heard from in almost two decades, most people assume that she is dead. Elizabeth's closest friends would still know her, thus the need for secrecy and caution."

Jacob continued on, "Okay, so that means that you, former captain of the royal guards, through marriage to Queen Mary Elizabeth of Avondale, are the actual king of Avondale?"

"I've never really thought of it that way, but I suppose the answer is yes," Raoul replied while looking carefully at his amazed visitors. "Believe me, I have no desire to be king. I am quite happy with my life of seclusion."

"Which would mean that King Humphrey and Queen Millicent aren't the real monarchs of the land and that their daughter isn't—" Jacob stopped speaking and looked at Catherine.

For a moment all was silent as Raoul and Jacob waited for Catherine to say something. There were definitely thoughts racing through her head, that much was obvious. How she would react to all of this new information, however, was a mystery.

Finally Catherine spoke. "So that explains the sword then!"

"The sword?" replied Jacob and Raoul at the exact same time.

"Raoul's sword…the one that Jacob described to me, the one with the royal crest. It has the same coat of arms that I saw on the banner in the secret room. You must have that sword because you were the captain of the guards," Catherine pointed out.

"Actually, that isn't rightfully my sword at all," confessed Raoul as he stood and walked over toward the door. "This was the king's sword, and he gave it to me when he was near death and asked me to keep it safe. It seemed very important to him, so I have taken the responsibility seriously." Raoul picked up the sword and carried it back to the table, placing it directly in front of Jacob and Catherine.

Jacob and the princess began admiring the fine workmanship of the sword. Its blade was broad and sharp without a single nick along its razor edge. The hilt was composed of a smooth, flawless handle with a pommel at its base for balance and a shiny silver quillion that served to protect the bearer's hands in battle. They both turned their attention to the coat of arms that was carved into the shoulder of the blade just above the quillion. It was, in fact, an intricate carving of the exact crest that Catherine studied in the castle's secret room.

"What do the animals represent?" asked Catherine to nobody in particular as she studied the remarkable detail of the hawk, bear, lion, fish, and wolf.

"I've often wondered that myself," replied Raoul.

"That crest has represented the royal throne of Avondale for many, many generations," said Elizabeth as she entered the room. Upon hearing her voice, Raoul, Jacob, and Catherine all quickly stood up. Raoul walked across the room, took her hand in his, and led her carefully to an empty chair at the table. They all sat down to continue their conversation.

"I suppose you have told them who I am?" questioned Elizabeth as she glanced at Raoul.

He simply nodded.

Elizabeth continued, "Even Rowland didn't seem to know the meaning of the crest. We just knew that its origin went back many hundreds of years. In fact, that engraving on the sword must be the original coat of arms, since the sword itself has been passed down to its rightful heir for generation after generation."

"This sword is an ancient heirloom?" Catherine gasped with delight as she turned it over to see the other side of the hilt.

"Something is missing here at the bottom." Jacob pointed to an oval recess at the base of the pommel.

"The sword has been like that for as long as I can remember," Elizabeth replied. "Rowland seemed unconcerned by its absence, but I always felt that it lost much of its beauty and value since it was no longer whole."

"Catherine! Look at the color of the hilt!" Jacob cried out. "It is dark blue!"

"And the shape of the missing object in the pommel!" Catherine exclaimed.

Jacob quickly reached his hand behind his neck, pulled the long drawstring over his head, and withdrew the silk pouch from beneath his shirt. Fumbling with the drawstring, he opened the pouch and gently tipped it upside down, holding it just above the table. Out slid the brilliant oval gem onto the table top, and to Jacob's surprise, a small, intricate, golden, figurine in the shape of a lion also hit the wooden table with a slight clink.

"Your reason for escape?" Raoul questioned while slowly shaking his head in disbelief. "Is there anything else you've failed to mention?"

Jacob gave a contrite smile and shrugged his shoulders innocently. Without saying a word, he picked up the priceless gem and placed it in the oval recess of the sword's pommel. As soon as he did so a powerful light, just like the one that had injured the jester's hand, flashed brightly out from the entire length of the sword, causing them to turn their heads and shield their eyes.

After a moment or two of temporary blindness, Jacob and the others regained their vision and once again stared at the wondrous sword. It seemed to Jacob to be even more magnificent than before. It was as if the blade itself glowed because of its brilliance. The hilt was now even richer and deeper in color, and the gem fit seamlessly in its new position. Even the carving of the coat of arms was different. The detail seemed greater and more intricate, and the minute animals were more lifelike to Jacob's eyes.

Remembering the figurine on the table in front of him, Jacob picked up the little golden lion, studying it carefully. It had a long, flowing mane and strong, powerful limbs and looked as if it was standing on its hind legs with its forepaws reaching out in front. Jacob could see that it was the same size and shape as the lion carved into the blade, so he reached over and put it into its place in the coat of arms.

The sound of a thunderous lion's roar suddenly echoed throughout the small room.

CHAPTER 20

The small figurine melded into the shoulder of the blade. The lion was now golden in color and flush with the blade's surface, while all of the other animals in the crest were still imprinted engravings.

Jacob looked up at the others and said quite loudly, his ears still buzzing, "That was interesting."

"Interesting?" asked Catherine. "I feel as if I've stared into the sun for an hour straight, my ears are still ringing from a deafening lion's roar, and we are looking at a sword that is centuries old that has magical properties, and all you can say is 'That was interesting'?"

"Jacob, where did you get that pouch and its contents?" asked the wide-eyed former captain. "I fear Ambrose more than ever now."

"It's a long story, but one that I am excited to tell. I'm sure that Catherine can fill in some of the gaps along the way."

"I'm sure she will," Raoul replied with a smile.

"I'll try and listen while I make us some dinner," Elizabeth said as she stood and walked toward the small pantry. She began gathering ingredients for potato soup and fresh bread.

Jacob, with Catherine's help, proceeded to tell all about the excitement they had experienced over the last couple of days. They described the skull and gem, the affect it had over Jacob, the other artifacts in the secret room, the conversation between the king and jester—Catherine told that part—and how the gem had burnt the jester's hand when he touched it. Raoul asked many questions along the way, and it seemed to Jacob that he was enjoying the story very much.

Even Elizabeth interrupted two or three times during the account while busily preparing the food. She explained how the skull and gem had been in the upper room for as long as she could remember. "It's at least as old as the sword is," she said at one point when she heard the others talking about its possible age.

At another point in the conversation she said, "I didn't like seeing the skull sitting there on the shelf, so I rarely went into that room. We never kept anything else in there while we lived there, and it was always locked. Rowland didn't speak often about the skull, but I had a feeling that he knew something more about its origin. Maybe its secret was passed down from king to king over the years. He did spend many days in quiet conversation with his father as it became obvious that his father's days were limited. Rowland was a lot like him. He was a good man and a great king in his own right."

Eventually the story was finished. Jacob had even described his escape from the castle.

Catherine, who had been absent during some of the escape and hadn't heard all of the details yet herself, said, "Jacob, are you sure you aren't embellishing a little bit? You actually kicked food all over Millicent and then completed a flip off of the table and landed on your feet behind Humphrey and the jester?"

"Yes, but I can see why you would have a hard time believing it. It happened automatically. My fear of being caught must have helped me escape, because I was running faster and jumping higher than I ever have before."

"And why did the gem burn the jester's hand?" asked Raoul quietly.

"More curious than that is why didn't it burn mine, and why was I able to lift the skull in the first place?"

"And why did it put Jacob into a trance, whereas I was not affected at all?" questioned Catherine.

Raoul looked at Elizabeth, who was now approaching the table with arms full of piping-hot soup and fresh, warm bread and caught her gaze. She shook her head from side to side almost imperceptibly as she placed the food down and turned back for dishes and spoons.

Jacob and Catherine, who hadn't noticed the odd exchange between Raoul and Elizabeth, continued on with unanswered questions.

After Elizabeth returned with the dishes and they all started sipping the hot soup and eating the fresh bread, there was a long silence. As they ate quietly, each one of them was deep in thought about the events of the last few days.

After everyone had finished their food, Raoul explained to the others that he wanted to be sure that Ambrose and the other guards were not approaching the cottage. He knew the area well and could easily slip through the forest toward the main road without detection and without leaving any tracks behind. It was no longer raining, and the sky had mostly cleared, and if he hurried he would just make it back before the setting of the sun.

Catherine busied herself by helping Elizabeth clean up the dishes and pots and leftover food.

Jacob needed more time to sit and think quietly about how to avoid being captured and killed—or worse yet, locked up in the dungeons for the rest of his life. More than that, he was worried about the safety of Catherine, Raoul, and Elizabeth. After following Raoul outside, Jacob collapsed onto a sturdy wooden chair on the porch. His shoulders felt heavy.

"I won't be more than an hour," Raoul said as he glanced back at Jacob. "If you see me running toward you when I return, gather the women and the sword, and we will try and escape into the forest."

"Okay, but are you sure you don't want to take the sword with you?"

"After your description of the jester's deformed hand, I'm not sure that I dare touch the sword ever again. It would be best if you kept it near you at all times."

"I'll get it then and bring it out here with me." Jacob walked toward the cottage door so he could retrieve it.

"The scabbard is in the bedroom." Raoul turned and disappeared into the thickest part of the forest.

When Jacob entered the cottage the kitchen was mostly cleaned up, and Catherine and Elizabeth were talking happily and smiling. Elizabeth had lit an oil lantern that was hanging from the low ceiling above the table. It cast a warm glow over the cozy little room.

Catherine looked over at Jacob and said, "You never told me how much fun it is cleaning and scrubbing pots and pans."

"You think *that* is fun, wait until you try a chamber pot. You will never want to do anything else with your time!" Jacob replied with a grin as he reached the table and grabbed the hilt of King Rowland's sword.

As he did so Jacob saw an inscription of some kind appear along the surface of the brilliant blade. He was startled by the writing, and he quickly pulled his hand back. The words vanished. His curiosity peaked, Jacob reached out and touched the hilt again. The writing reappeared.

"Catherine! Come and see this!"

"What is it?" asked Catherine as she and Elizabeth appeared at his side a few seconds later.

"When I touch the sword this writing appears, and when I let go it vanishes," Jacob pointed out excitedly. He did it again to show the women what would happen.

Catherine, reached out her own hand and touched the sword's hilt.

"Nothing happened," Jacob said curiously.

"That's exactly what I expected, Jacob! You're the only one who was affected by the gem's power. No one else could lift the skull or remove the gem from its forehead. And this sword only responds to your touch. Touch it again."

Jacob did so, and when the writing materialized this time Elizabeth leaned forward and said, "It's an inscription of some kind…a poem or a verse." She began to read it aloud.

The time has come, as was foretold, when monarchs care for naught but gold,

And wicked hearts will guide their reign as riches they strive to obtain.

But one will rise, who is just and true, and overcome the loathsome two.

And peace he'll bring to Avondale as is written in the ancient tale.

To everyone's surprise, the old verse faded away, and a new one appeared as soon as Elizabeth read the last word. Elizabeth continued reading:

From centuries past, I guide thee now with writ upon this ancient blade.

An arduous task you now will face—yet a path before you has been laid.

Each creature's skill you must obtain, the lion first and last the bear,

To gain the prowess you will need, to claim the throne as rightful heir.

Jacob slowly pulled his hand back after Elizabeth read the last line. The writing faded again.

"Rightful heir? What does this mean?" he asked aloud, although he already knew the answer. He looked at Catherine and then slowly turned to Elizabeth. A tear ran down her right cheek.

"I thought you were dead, Jacob."

CHAPTER 21

Jacob's mind was reeling from this sudden revelation. All of the seemingly amazing pieces of information that he had learned that day paled in comparison to this new understanding.

"You are my mother?" asked Jacob, not really expecting an answer.

"Is it really true, Elizabeth?" Catherine clapped her hands together excitedly and smiled.

As Jacob stood there, pondering this new awakening in his heart, the faceless images of his mother that would never materialize in his mind for as long as he could remember began to take form. Just as before, Jacob could remember a soft, smiling face looking down on him kindly —only this time the blurriness faded, and the gentle face focused into the recognizable countenance of the woman standing before him.

Jacob was full of mixed emotions. He was happy that his mother was alive and well but sad that he had grown up without real parents. Anger about being abandoned was quickly replaced with contentment as he realized that a different life would have meant a life without Catherine.

Stepping forward, Jacob embraced his mother warmly, and they both wept freely. After a moment, Catherine, who couldn't help herself, joined in on the embrace, and the three of them stood there together without speaking for a very long time.

"We seem safe for now," announced Raoul as he swung open the cottage door.

The sudden break in silence startled Jacob, Catherine, and Elizabeth so much that they quickly released each other and turned toward the door, wiping their eyes with their hands and sleeves.

"You told him?" Raoul guessed as he looked at his wife.

"Sort of," replied Elizabeth. "I guess you could say the sword told him." Raoul looked very confused; all at once Jacob and both women began speaking excitedly, trying to explain what had happened.

Raoul shouted, "Jacob, why don't *you* tell me what happened?" The room fell silent again.

Jacob explained the sword's mysterious inscriptions and told Raoul what they had learned.

When Jacob was finished, Raoul said, "We will talk about the sword again later on, but I suppose that you now know how I guessed your name the other day and why Elizabeth fainted when she saw you this morning."

"You knew who I was when you saw me? How did you know my name?" asked Jacob, sounding a little upset. "You said that we had never met."

"As for the name, Humphrey and Millicent did not give it to you. Your mother did. She had decided that you would be called Jacob long before you were born, if you were a boy," answered Raoul. "I told the orphanage that was your name, and they wrote it on your record. As for having never met, I suppose we did meet the day you were born. That *does* count, doesn't it?"

"Both Jacob and I tend to take things very literally, as you can see," Catherine conceded with a slight smile.

Raoul continued, "Now, as for recognizing you, you look very much like your father did when he was your age. I was his friend and captain. It was obvious to me the moment I saw you. And judging by Elizabeth's reaction earlier, it must have been obvious to her also."

"Raoul, you knew that my son was alive two days ago and didn't tell me?" asked Elizabeth with a mixture of disbelief and anger.

"Elizabeth, dear, I was waiting for the right time…I wanted it to be a surprise. Besides, if I would have told you sooner you would have stormed the castle looking for him, risking revealing your true identity and perhaps even your life…and Jacob's also."

"It seems that every answer I receive today carries with it even more questions," Jacob said quietly.

"I will give you whatever answers I can," responded Elizabeth. "It will be a long story, but you deserve to hear it. Why don't we sit down again?"

After they all found a place around the table, Elizabeth, who was sitting next to Jacob, looked directly at him and began telling her story.

"Rowland and I were very excited to learn that we were expecting our first child. Other than the physician in Strathwick, Sir Wilmot, we didn't tell a single person. We were hoping to make a grand announcement throughout Avondale. Soon after we found out, however, Rowland became very ill, and his health deteriorated rapidly. Sir Wilmot was quite puzzled by the sudden onset of the disease, and despite trying various treatments and remedies, he was unable to improve your father's condition in any way.

"It was apparent that Rowland would soon die, and I was devastated. I couldn't bear the thought of losing him, and I became very depressed. In fact, the only thing that kept my mind sane was the knowledge that my growing child was going to need me. One day, Rowland called Raoul and me to his bedside. He made me promise to leave the castle and raise our child as a commoner so that he or she could grow up without the pressures of the monarchy. He then asked Raoul to promise to watch over and protect me and our child and to keep us safe."

"That's when he gave me the sword," Raoul explained.

Elizabeth went on, "Lastly, he instructed us to tell no one that I was carrying a child and explained that he had also sworn the physician to secrecy. We were told that when the time came we were to trust only him with the delivery of my baby. We agreed. My dear Rowland died the next day."

Elizabeth paused briefly before continuing. "As promised, following the funeral Raoul and I left the castle without telling a single person. A bit of a recluse anyway"—Elizabeth turned and smiled at Raoul before continuing—"Raoul had already started work on this cottage, and it seemed like the perfect place to get away from all that had happened. Over the following months our days were spent finishing the cottage and preparing this home and our lives for your arrival." She smiled at Jacob.

"As the months passed by, Raoul eventually stopped calling me Your Highness or Queen Mary and slowly learned to use my middle name, which we both agreed I should be called. I still missed Rowland very much each and every day, but as time passed Raoul and I began to fall in love. His large stature is matched only by his kind and gentle nature. He protected and watched over me at first out of duty, and then out of love.

"I learned to enjoy the simple life here in the cottage, free from the pressures and worries of ruling and governing the whole kingdom. I even enjoyed the satisfaction of doing my own cooking and cleaning.

"But, as the day of your arrival grew nearer, I began to feel as if something was wrong. I soon grew feverish and weak and suffered more pain than I expected. When I mentioned this to Raoul, we immediately left for Strathwick. A day later when we finally arrived, my condition was dire. Sir Wilmot recognized me immediately and quickly went to work. Thankfully, he was able to help with your birth, and it seemed that I would recover well.

"I can still remember holding you in my arms, looking into your curious eyes, and feeling more love and happiness than I could have possibly imagined before you came into my life. However, the following day my health turned poor once again. My fever grew even worse than before, and I began to tremble and shake. I couldn't eat or drink for nourishment, and the physician soon became certain that I wouldn't live much longer without a specific herbal remedy. Afraid to leave my side, he sent Raoul to Dalcaster to buy the herbs and ointments that he needed to treat my condition."

"But that's a journey of two or three days in one direction," Catherine said. "How did Raoul return in time?"

Raoul answered, "Yes, Catherine, you are correct. There was no time to lose. Elizabeth was in no condition to care for her new child, and the physician was concentrating all of his efforts on her illness. I needed to hurry to Dalcaster immediately and couldn't watch over an infant either, so I did what I thought was the proper choice and took him to the orphanage.

"I explained to the woman there that I had no other choice but to leave this new child in her care for a short time. I told her that his name was Jacob and that I would return to get him as soon as possible. After paying a small amount of money and signing a false name on the record, I sped to Dalcaster as quickly as my horse could take me. Even without stopping for more than a few minutes at a time to rest my horse, it took me just over two days to reach the city. It was late evening when I finally arrived."

"You must have been exhausted!" exclaimed Catherine.

"Yes, I was," replied Raoul. "And very hungry also, although my horse was worse off than I, and it was obvious that he couldn't possibly carry me back to Strathwick quickly enough. I found an inn with a corral where I obtained food and lodging for the evening and where I slept fitfully until early morning. Immediately after awakening I left the inn, sold my horse to a nearby peasant farmer, and left for the market street.

"Just a short time later I located and purchased all of the herbs and other supplies that were necessary and acquired a new horse to get me back to Strathwick quickly. It was a young yet well-trained courser stallion, and I paid handsomely for him. He was swift and strong. I rode quickly out of the city and hurried back toward Strathwick with great speed. As before, my stops were brief, and in less than two days I was once again sitting by Elizabeth's side."

"And it was a good thing," said Elizabeth, "as my condition had worsened during Raoul's absence. Sir Wilmot worked quickly as he mixed various remedies of ointments and broths using the supplies that Raoul purchased."

Raoul continued, "Elizabeth did not awaken for many days, and there were times that I was certain she was knocking on death's door. Eventually, the fever began to subside, and the pain and swelling decreased."

Elizabeth interrupted again, "I remember waking up from what seemed like a very long dream, turning my head, and seeing Raoul sitting by the side of my bed. 'Raoul,' I said, 'please bring Jacob to me so that I may hold him again.'

"I saw tears form instantly in Raoul's eyes and then slowly run down his cheeks. He was silent and didn't move.

"I pleaded with him, 'Raoul, please bring him to me. I want to see him.'

"Raoul took a deep breath and said, 'Elizabeth, dear, I am sorry, but I can't. Jacob is dead.'

"When I heard those awful words, I lost my will to live. The pain and sorrow that poured down upon me was equal in strength to the love and happiness that I had felt at your birth. I entered a profound depression that I did not escape for years to come. I had lost my son."

CHAPTER 22

"Raoul! Why did you tell her that I was dead?" Jacob asked before standing from the table and positioning the chair back to its proper place. He began slowly pacing the floor.

"Because until two days ago I believed it to be true!" Raoul affirmed. "When I returned from Dalcaster, I went straight to the physician and delivered the supplies that he needed to begin his treatments. Then, despite my hunger and lack of sleep, I went directly to the orphanage to get you. When I arrived and asked the woman to bring you to me, she began acting very strangely.

"She said that she didn't remember me or a child named Jacob that had been admitted. I became angry and demanded to see all of the children at once. The woman nervously obliged, but as I entered the room where all of the children were kept, there wasn't a single newborn to be found among the numerous other orphans. Worriedly, I asked to see the document that I had signed. The woman was gone for quite some time, but finally she returned with the paper.

"She slowly handed it to me. 'I remember now, sir,' she said with a quivering voice. 'The young boy that you brought here became ill soon after you left. We did what we could, but I am afraid…' Her voice trailed off.

"I looked down at the paper in my hand, and written on the top of the page was the word *deceased*.

"'How did this happen?' I questioned her angrily. 'Not five days ago I left him here, and he was healthy and well!'

"'Sir, I am sorry, but he became sick soon after you left. We couldn't do anything for him,' the woman answered nervously.

"'The body then. Give me the body so he can have a proper burial,' I demanded.

"'Once again, sir, forgive me, but I am afraid that I can't. Sickness and death are not rare things in the orphanage recently. Now that King Humphrey sits on the throne, we have many more children to care for, and he provides very little food and supplies. We can only bury the bodies in a single large grave outside of the city walls. I truly am sorry,' she replied. 'We never expected your return. You see, children are often left in our care with promises of return. You are the first to come back for your child.'

"I had nothing left to say or do, so I turned and left. I went to Elizabeth's side, not knowing if she would live or die, but knowing that if she did live I would be the one to tell her about the loss of her son. I had fallen in love with her and had hoped to raise her child as my own. As the days of her recovery passed, I dreaded the time when I would have to relay the news of Jacob's, I mean, your death.

"As you have already heard, she took it very badly. It took years for her heavy heart to slowly mend. And to make matters worse, the birth and its related illness had taken a heavy toll on her body. She was no longer able to have children."

"Humphrey and Millicent must have come and taken me while you were traveling to and from Dalcaster," Jacob responded softly. He slid out his chair and once again took his place at the table.

"I have thought that very thing for the last two days," Raoul replied. "I can only imagine that the woman there was threatened with the dungeons or paid handsomely for her part."

"Threatened, I would say," Catherine surmised. "Humphrey wouldn't readily give up his gold if he could avoid it." Reaching over, she placed her soft hand on top of Jacob's and gave a gentle squeeze.

"Why would they choose me out of all of the other orphans?" Jacob asked. "There must have been some older boys who could have been taken and raised as a servant in the castle."

Elizabeth answered, "Millicent would have chosen an infant if one was available. A newborn child would have been too irresistible for her to leave behind."

Especially since she was unable to have children of her own, Catherine thought, wondering if then was the right time for her own surprising fact. But she hesitated for some reason.

"Jacob, I am sorry that I wasn't able to be with you and watch you grow over the years, but I'm grateful that you are alive, and I feel blessed that you are here with me now," Elizabeth said with tears in her eyes as she leaned over and embraced him.

"It is good to know that I was loved and the circumstances of my adoption. I'm very happy to have a mother and to be free from Humphrey and Millicent. This has been the best day of my entire life without question," Jacob replied with a warm smile. His watery eyes glistened, reflecting light from the oil lantern hanging from the ceiling.

After a long silence, Jacob stood from the table again and said boldly, "Well, I have a kingdom to overthrow!"

PART II

AVONDALE

CHAPTER 23

"Before you go storming the castle, let's remember the inscription on the sword." Elizabeth reached up, grabbed Jacob's arm, and gently pulled him back into his seat. "It spoke of a task that you need to complete to gain the abilities of each of the animals in the coat of arms."

"The lion first and last the bear!" exclaimed Catherine. "Don't you see, Jacob? We need to find the figurines representing the other four animals now—you already have the lion!"

"If I already have a lion's ability, why don't I feel any differently right now?" questioned Jacob. He looked down at the backs of his hands, wondering what he might see.

"I don't know, but it seems that you *did* feel differently when you escaped from the castle. The changes are likely to be subtle. You were able to run faster and jump higher than ever before. After all, you don't expect to actually turn into a lion, do you?" asked Catherine.

"I don't know what to expect!" Jacob replied a little more harshly than he intended. "A few hours ago I was just an orphan servant boy cleaning out chamber pots and smelling your mother's stinky shoes! Now I am sitting next to my long-lost mother as an heir to the throne, and I have just learned that it is my destiny to bring peace to the entire kingdom of Avondale! For all I know, I *will* turn into a lion at any moment!" Jacob added, his voice escalating.

"Millicent is *not* my mother!" Catherine blurted. "How do you think I feel, Jacob? I have gone from princess to orphan in the same amount of time it took for you to become royalty. You may have found your mother, but I have lost mine." Tears formed in her eyes.

"Not your mother?" questioned Jacob, speaking softly. "What do you mean Millicent is not your mother?"

"Blythe told me," Catherine divulged quietly as she glanced down. "I just found out myself. The servants have known all along, but they were threatened with their lives not to tell anyone."

"So that's why she wanted to speak with you the other day," guessed Jacob. He felt ashamed of how he had spoken just moments before.

"Truthfully, I wasn't as surprised by Blythe's words as you might think. I've never felt any real closeness with Humphrey and Millicent. Besides, you probably haven't noticed, but I don't really bear a family resemblance," Catherine said with a slight smile. She lifted her head up and looked at the others again.

Elizabeth reached across the table and took Catherine's hand in hers. "You are a beautiful and intelligent young woman. You have many dear friends who love you and would give their lives for you if necessary. Your kind demeanor and innate goodness are a part of who you are, no matter your birthright."

"Thank you," replied Catherine through a tearful smile. Then in an obvious attempt to change the subject, she said, "The sword then, Jacob. Touch it again so we can get on with your, I mean *our* quest."

Jacob smiled as he reached over and pulled the sword to the table's center. As before, an inscription appeared along the surface of the blade. Raoul, who was noticeably pleased to be involved with the mysterious writing this time, began reading the verse.

Seek the winged beast that doth ride the breeze,

And nests on Avondale's king of trees.

Look beneath the roost, the hawk to obtain,

And sight, not flight, ye then will gain.

As expected, when Raoul finished the last sentence the words disappeared. Jacob pulled his hand away briefly and then touched the sword again. Nothing happened.

"Just as I thought," Jacob said excitedly. "The next clue won't appear until I have completed this one."

"You mean until *we* have completed this one," added Catherine, putting her hand on her hips.

"Yes," stated Raoul, "*we* leave first thing in the morning."

"I won't be going," said Elizabeth. "I'm going to the castle instead."

"The castle!" exclaimed Jacob, Catherine, and Raoul all at once.

"Someone has to figure out what's happening there and what Ambrose is planning to do next, and it certainly cannot be one of you!" Elizabeth copied Catherine's expression, daring Raoul to disagree. He didn't, and she went on. "Besides, Catherine and I were supposed to have our usual lesson tomorrow anyway, and it seems that it wouldn't be wise for me to be absent. They might suspect something. Now let's have some supper and get some rest."

Elizabeth jumped from her chair and went over to the stove to begin preparing their evening meal before anyone could argue with her. Catherine smirked as the two men sat there speechlessly, knowing that there was no sense in arguing with either of the women.

"Tomorrow then," said Jacob.

Raoul nodded.

They ate and talked very little the rest of the evening. Everyone seemed nervous as they prepared provisions. Before long, emotional and physical exhaustion set in, and they realized they were ready for bed. Catherine and Elizabeth slept comfortably on the wool mattress in the bedroom, while the two men wrapped themselves in thick blankets and lay by the door on the wooden floor. Jacob kept his sword close by his side.

Throughout the long, dark night even the slightest creak or noise awakened Jacob from his sporadic sleep; he expected Ambrose and the other guards to come crashing through the door at any moment. The seemingly endless hours, however, eventually passed by uneventfully. Yet Jacob still didn't feel very well rested when morning came.

"You must have slept about as well as I did, Raoul," guessed Jacob after noticing the weariness in the older man's countenance.

They sat around the table and ate a breakfast of fresh bread, cheese, and milk.

"I have become soft in my old age it seems, or the floor has become harder than it was in my youth." Raoul laughed as he twisted his shoulders back and forth to stretch out his sore back. "I suppose we'll be sleeping on the ground for the next many weeks, however, so I'd better get used to it."

"So where do we go to find the hawk?" Jacob asked after swallowing a mouthful of food.

Catherine was the one who answered. "It would seem from the inscription on the sword that we are looking for a very tall tree. I think we should go toward Woodhurst. There must be someone there who could tell us where to find the king of trees."

"I agree," stated Raoul. "The forest is just as thick on this side of the wide valley, but the larger trees are found to the west. We *will* go to Woodhurst, and I have a plan that will allow Elizabeth to go to the castle and gain valuable information about the guards' plans and still join us on our journey."

"This is so exciting!" Catherine said while softly clapping her hands .

"And dangerous, Catherine. Don't let your desire for adventure affect your ability to be cautious and vigilant," warned Elizabeth. "We all need to avoid being recognized at all costs."

"Which will make my plan seem a bit absurd, I am afraid," Raoul said. "We will *all* go toward the castle as soon as possible."

"Toward the castle? All of us?" Jacob looked bewildered. "Have you gone mad? You need more sleep."

"I know it seems foolish, Jacob," Raoul replied. "But I had plenty of time to ponder our strategy during the night, and I think it is our best option at this point. Remember, I have served as captain of the guards, and I'm quite certain that Ambrose and his men are well on their way to Aberfield right now. If this kind of thing happened twenty years ago, I would have ridden straight through the night, despite the storm, to try and recover the princess of Avondale.

"In case I am wrong, I propose that we cross the road and river, travel west for a mile or two, and then journey straight southward. It will take more time than if we were to stay on the road, but we should be out of harm's way. When we approach Strathwick, Elizabeth can hurry to the castle, act as if she is there for the princess's lesson, and then meet us again to tell us about Ambrose's plans."

"That sounds reasonable," Catherine said. She tried very hard to sound as unenthusiastic as possible, but it didn't work.

"Okay then," said Jacob. "The sooner we obtain all of the figurines, the sooner we can be free from all of this worry."

"Yes, Jacob," replied Elizabeth with a smile, "and then comes the worry of ruling over a kingdom."

"Let's hope it comes to that," Raoul said. "It will be death or dungeons if we fail."

CHAPTER 24

A short time later the four adventurers found themselves quietly walking single file through the thick trees of the forest. The morning air was chilly, and the tips of the travelers' shoes were now quite wet from the rain-soaked vegetation and fallen leaves on the forest floor. Raoul was walking up front with his horse following directly behind him. Elizabeth and her black mare, then Catherine and Mabel, and lastly Jacob followed behind. Jacob's mind was fixed on the magnificent sword that was now sheathed at his left. He was proud to be wearing such a priceless and handsome weapon.

Saddling the horses and arranging the packs and supplies on their backs took longer than they had anticipated. To make matters worse, every time Jacob thought that they were ready to leave, Raoul would remember one more item that he decided was absolutely necessary for their trek to Woodhurst.

Jacob had grown quite impatient by the time Raoul finally closed the cottage door for the last time and stated, "Okay, that should do."

"Are you sure this time?" questioned Jacob. "You have gone back in there more times than I can remember."

"Be patient. You will be glad that I brought many of these items at some point during this journey. The flint is for fire, the crossbow for hunting food, and the canvas for shelter."

"I'm sorry. I am just nervous about this whole adventure. I guess I just want to get started so that it can be over with sooner."

As Jacob was walking alone at the back of the procession, he found himself already grateful for Raoul's experience and knowledge. Jacob had escaped the castle with nothing but the clothes that he was wearing, a mysterious blue gem, and a lion figurine that he didn't even know he had at the time. Raoul's expertise would prove to be invaluable on this journey—of that Jacob was certain.

After a while the traveling party reached the broader part of the trail, and Catherine and Jacob were able to walk side by side and speak to each other about the task at hand.

"I have always wanted to see the rest of the kingdom, but this isn't exactly what I had in mind," said Jacob. "I am quite certain that I would enjoy these travels just a bit more if I wasn't being hunted." After a brief pause he added, "I have a feeling that this trip to Woodhurst will not be easy."

"I think the most difficult part will be finding the correct tree," Catherine replied in an attempt to put Jacob's mind at ease.

"Or climbing it once we find it." Jacob nervously looked up at the tops of the trees all around him. "I can't imagine it being much taller than these trees are." There was a hint of hope in his voice.

"Someone had to climb the tree and hide the figurine up there in the first place. I am sure that you will be okay."

"That was a long time ago. The tree has certainly grown taller since then," said Jacob.

Another minute or two of near silence passed by. Only the sounds of their footfalls and the breathing of the horses were just slightly audible in the quiet of the forest.

"Who do you think it was?" Jacob finally asked. "Someone went through a lot of effort to hide the figurines and prepare the gem and sword for their roles in all of this."

"We'll probably never know, but it had to be someone who could see the future and work magic. I would guess that he was one of your ancestors from centuries past."

"Why didn't he just put all of the other figurines into the pouch with the lion? I could have overtaken the king right then and there and saved us from all of this effort and worry."

"I don't think that is how it works. There's a reason why the task is not an easy one. I think there are things that you will learn about yourself along the way that will prepare you to be the king of Avondale. Besides, if the figurines *had* been placed all together in the silk pouch and the jester would have been able to break the skull, then he might have gained all of the animals' abilities. That would have been terrible!"

"I guess you're right. Besides, I wouldn't want to deprive you of all this fun you are having," Jacob said with a smile.

Before she could reply, Catherine walked right into the back of Elizabeth's mare. Jacob and Catherine had been speaking so intently that they hadn't even noticed that Raoul and Elizabeth had come to an abrupt halt just up ahead. Raoul had a disapproving look on his face. When Jacob's eyes met his, the brawny man sternly motioned for the young adventurers to be quiet.

Jacob answered with an apologetic nod.

Raoul's face softened. He handed his horse's reins to Elizabeth and then motioned for the others to stay still and wait quietly. They had nearly reached the forest's edge, and he wanted to make sure that they would not be seen by anyone traveling to or from Aberfield. He then turned and slowly crept forward until he was standing just inside the last row of trees. After listening intently for the sounds of human voices or the steady fall of horses' hooves on the ground, Raoul decided that it was safe, and he stepped slowly out of the forest and onto the road. After glancing to make sure that they were not in any danger of being discovered, he whistled for the others to join him.

When Jacob and the women arrived at Raoul's side, he was crouched down and studying the dirt road carefully. After a few seconds he stood and asked, "How far ahead of the guards were you when you entered the forest yesterday?"

"An hour at least, maybe more," answered Jacob.

"And the storm? When did it begin to rain?"

"Just as we entered the forest. It rained very hard for ten or fifteen minutes and then lightly for another ten minutes after that. Is something the matter?"

"Yesterday when I left the cottage to make sure that we were safe, I came all the way to where we are standing right now. There were no visible tracks anywhere on the road, and I felt confident that you and Catherine had not been followed. I assumed that the guards were still tracking you but had not yet passed by here. Now, there are a fair number of tracks heading toward Aberfield. They were left by the guards, as can be seen by the crest stamped into the horses' shoes. However, they are fresh and not as numerous as I would have expected. We need Elizabeth to find out why so few men have been sent to capture you and why they delayed their search until this morning."

"There still may be more guards to come, Raoul. We should cross the road and river and get out of sight as quickly as we can," suggested Elizabeth.

"Yes, dear, I agree. But I must do something first."

Raoul withdrew a large folding knife from a pack on his horse and walked over to Mabel. After picking up her back left foot, he stepped over the leg and held the mare's hoof steadily between his knees. Using the sturdy knife, he carefully pushed the sharp point between the hoof and the massive shoe and pried it up and down. In less than a minute the shoe and all of its nails had been wrestled from the large hoof. Raoul then turned his attention to the other three shoes, and before long the chore was accomplished.

After placing the heavy horseshoes into his pack, he said, "Quickly now, mount your horses and follow me."

Jacob jumped onto Mabel's back and pulled Catherine up behind him. When he looked forward again, Raoul and Elizabeth had already started across the road. Lightly kicking his heels into Mabel's sides, Jacob urged her forward.

The three horses carried their masters across the dirt road and through the meandering river without hesitation, and soon they were galloping westward over rolling hills of wildflowers and lush green grasses on the plains of Avondale. There were occasional farmsteads with fields of crops and livestock scattered about, but the travelers stayed a fair distance away from the dwellings in order to avoid being noticed. After a mile or two Raoul slowed his horse to a walk and turned to the south. The others caught up and rode alongside.

"It's late morning already. Elizabeth will soon be overdue for her lesson, and we are still a long way from Strathwick," Raoul said.

"I've been late before," replied Elizabeth, "but it would be better if we hurried as quickly as possible."

"Then let us ride swiftly," answered Raoul as his spurred his horse into a run.

It took the traveling party a few hours to reach the outskirts of Strathwick. Raoul discovered a small grove of trees situated just a few hundred yards north of the large town's outer wall. They all agreed that it was a good location for hiding and waiting while Elizabeth rode to the castle and back.

Jacob secretly hoped that they would be able to go into Strathwick and do some wandering around. He knew that it was far too dangerous because of the risk of being discovered, but he had never been to any of the towns or villages in Avondale, and he had heard that Strathwick was the grandest of them all.

He had also been told by the other castle servants that there was a tall rock wall surrounding the entire township except for the two entrances, one on the eastern end of the town and the other to the west. The road between the Castleford Bridge and the village of Woodhurst bisected Strathwick as it passed through the center of the settlement and through each of the entryways.

Every evening at each of these entrances, large, sturdy gates were swung together and locked with stout chains and padlocks. Sentries were posted all through the night to keep watch over the city so that its inhabitants could sleep peacefully. Just thinking about the mysteries of Strathwick and knowing that he was standing such a short distance away made Jacob even more anxious to go and explore.

"I'll ride with Elizabeth to the bridge and then return," Raoul explained to Jacob and Catherine. "You two stay here and avoid being seen or heard. I'll be back shortly." He and his wife turned their horses eastward and galloped away.

Jacob looked at Catherine, and with boredom in his voice said, "Well, which tree do you want to lean against? I'll let you have the first choice."

"Lean against? Maybe you should practice climbing." Catherine laughed. "Try that one over there." She pointed to a tall tree growing near the edge of the small grove.

"That's not a bad idea." Jacob strolled over to the base of the tree and looked upward at its first large branch. It was well above his head.

"I wasn't being serious, Jacob. You might get hurt."

"If I get injured while climbing this one, I have no business scaling Avondale's king of trees." Jacob crouched down slightly and pushed hard off the ground. Much more easily than he anticipated, he reached the tall branch, grasped it strongly with both hands, and swung himself up onto the thick limb. He looked down at Catherine and smiled.

"That was amazing!" Catherine exclaimed. "That didn't even seem possible, yet you did it so effortlessly."

Feeling quite confident, Jacob looked up at the next branch and pushed off with his legs again. This time, he leapt skillfully from branch to branch, and soon he was crouched on a small limb near the very top of the tree. After looking down at Catherine for the second time, he yelled, "I'm not as worried about finding the hawk as I was a minute ago!"

Catherine seemed envious that Jacob was perched so high in a tree and able to look out in all directions. "What can you see from up there?"

After straightening himself up into an almost-standing position, Jacob surveyed the area around him. Although the tree was tall enough for him to see over the outer wall of the city, he was unable to make out anything in much detail.

He shouted back down to Catherine, "I can tell that Strathwick is larger than I expected, and there are many houses and buildings, but other than that I can't see very much!"

"What about the river? How far are we from the bridge?"

Looking toward the east, Jacob could just see the meandering river's wavy blue line in the distance. There were lush fields of green all around it, and he thought he could see the Castleford Bridge as it spanned the shimmering water a few miles away. Once again Jacob was frustrated with the lack of detail in his sight. Even the large castle that he knew so well was just a dot of blurry stonework in the distance. Yet he *could* see that not far from the tree where he stood was a single rider on a horse galloping in his direction.

"Raoul is coming back!" Jacob shouted down to Catherine.

Before she could reply, he began descending the sturdy tree. In a matter of seconds he landed gracefully on both feet after completing a back flip off the lowest branch.

"Now you are just showing off," Catherine said, rolling her eyes again.

Jacob smiled. "Sorry, I'm just trying to get used to my new abilities."

Just then Raoul rode into the grove and dismounted his horse. "Now we wait. And this time let's do so quietly."

Elizabeth was anxious as she lifted and then let go of the large iron door knocker at the castle's main entrance. She had always felt nervous about being recognized as she came to tutor the princess, but this time she was actually afraid. For a moment she considered turning around and asking Ossian's replacement to open the gate again so that she could leave and never return. Realizing that she needed information in order to help keep Catherine, her husband, and her son safe from capture, she swung the heavy knocker down once again. Moments later the stout door opened slowly and revealed another of the king's guards. Elizabeth recognized the tall, intimidating guard from her previous trips to the castle.

"I'm sorry that I'm late for the princess's lesson. I had an errand to run in Strathwick before coming here, and it took longer than I expected," Elizabeth quickly said without revealing her nervousness. "I do hope that the queen isn't displeased with me," she added when the guard didn't offer to escort her to the drawing room, as was customary.

"You may enter if you like, but there will be no lesson today," answered the brutish guard as he moved sideways to allow room for Elizabeth to step into the entry hall. "I will ask whether or not the queen would like to see you." Elizabeth waited for what must have been five or ten minutes, trying unsuccessfully to avoid staring at the awful portraits hanging above her, but finally Queen Millicent came shuffling heavily around the corner. She was wiping the corners of her mouth with an elaborate napkin and chewing quickly in an attempt to force down whatever lump of food was in her mouth. She had swollen red eyes and a melancholy complexion. She approached Elizabeth, threw her arms around her, and began to sob uncontrollably.

Elizabeth, who had always disliked the current queen for the way she treated others, felt a pang of remorse. This woman, as detestable as she was, had lost her only child, and Elizabeth could sympathize. With guilt in her heart, she gently pushed the queen away so that she could look into her eyes. She asked softly, "Your Highness, what is the matter? What has caused you this much grief?"

Millicent, who was now using the beautiful napkin as a handkerchief, trumpeted her nose as cleanly as she could, took one last swallow to clear her throat, and answered, "My Catherine has been kidnapped." She began bawling again.

Unable to be heard over her wailing, Elizabeth took Millicent by the hand and escorted her down the dim corridor to their right. Turning left as they approached the staircase, they went past Catherine's room and then entered the drawing room. After helping the queen get settled into her new chair near the center of the room, Elizabeth took a seat on a couch directly across from her.

Sitting on the edge of the cushion, she leaned forward and said, "Your Highness, I need you to tell me what happened."

The directness in Elizabeth's voice seemed to separate the queen from her anguish enough to slow her tears and enable her to recount her version of the previous day's events. It took much longer than Elizabeth hoped it would, but eventually Millicent's tale was finished. Elizabeth had learned that the horrible servant boy, Jacob, had stolen much of their treasure, including her prized horse, ransacked the castle, and kidnapped the princess against her will.

Millicent herself had seen the princess kick and scream and fight with all her might to get away, but the strong young man had tied her up and thrown her roughly onto the horse before galloping away. Catherine had tried to express her immense love for the queen as the wretched Jacob boy took her away through the main gate, but she had been gagged with a rag or a cloth and was unable to be heard.

"He had an accomplice, you know," explained the queen as she was finishing up her story. "The one who was guarding the gate will rot in the dungeons for helping him escape."

"My Queen, what is being done to capture the servant, and do the guards have any ideas about the princess's whereabouts?" inquired Elizabeth when she was finally able to ask a question.

"He was heading north toward Aberfield when they began tracking him, but they couldn't overtake him, and the storm soon washed away the horse's tracks."

"So the guards returned?"

"Yes, but they left again at sunrise. Ambrose took a dozen men to Aberfield with him and also sent a few to Dalcaster, Strathwick, and Woodhurst. After they post notices and announce the princess's abduction throughout the kingdom, they are commanded to return to the castle for further instructions." The queen blew her nose loudly enough to make Elizabeth wince. "Ambrose will try and track them down as he travels northward. If he is unable to find them along the way, he will post drawings of Jacob all over Aberfield and then question the townspeople, roughly if necessary."

"A drawing? The notices have a drawing of Jacob on them?"

"Yes. The same artist who painted our grand portraits years ago agreed to come and work straight through the night. He portrayed him very well, actually."

"Well, Your Highness, I am afraid that I must leave now. I will pray for Catherine's safety. She is a wonderful young woman." Without waiting for a response from the queen, Elizabeth stood, bowed a quick good-bye, and left the drawing room, hurrying to the main doors. It wasn't long before she had made it out of the castle and through the main gate. As the heavy iron bars closed noiselessly behind her, she quickly mounted her horse that had been left tethered just outside of the castle grounds and galloped off toward Strathwick.

CHAPTER 25

"Raoul, don't you think it would be safe enough for me to enter Strathwick through the east gate, walk straight through town on the main road, leave through the west gate, and circle back here to the trees?" Jacob asked. "We have been waiting for nearly an hour."

Jacob had already climbed another tree, explored the entirety of the small grove around him, and practiced sheathing and unsheathing his sword multiple times. All the while Catherine was incessantly asking Raoul questions about the old times in Avondale when he was the captain of the guards. Raoul, patiently answered most of her questions, but it was obvious that he was nervous about his wife's safe return.

"It's too risky. Elizabeth will be here soon," replied Raoul.

"What about supplies? Don't we need any provisions before we start for Woodhurst?"

"No, we don't. Why do you think it took so long for us to leave the cottage this morning? I have everything we need to get us to Woodhurst, and we can replenish our supplies when we arrive there in three or four days. And although it may not fit as well as you might wish, we even have extra clothing for both you and Catherine." Raoul was ringing his calloused hands together nervously.

"Jacob, you'll have plenty of opportunities to see the kingdom when you are responsible for it. For now you need to keep safe enough to avoid capture and finish this task that has been given you," cautioned Catherine.

"Thank you, Catherine," said Raoul. "I'm not sure where that stroke of wisdom came from, considering that you too are generally seeking adventure more than you should."

Catherine smiled, but before she could counter with her own response, she heard the sound of a twig break just a few yards behind her. Jacob and Raoul jumped to their feet quickly.

Jacob unsheathed his powerful sword and held it out in front of him, while Raoul whispered as loudly as he dared, "Elizabeth, is that you?"

"Yes, Raoul, it is me," came the soft, nearly breathless reply.

Raoul, Catherine, and Jacob breathed a simultaneous sigh of relief as they recognized Elizabeth's tender voice. The kind face of Jacob's mother appeared from behind a clump of trees. She had her black horse in tow behind her. Her hair was windswept, and her reddish face looked fatigued.

"Did you encounter any trouble?" questioned Raoul. "You have been hurrying, I see."

"No difficulties, but I have some information that is quite troubling." She inhaled deeply to catch her breath.

Elizabeth went on to recount her whole conversation with the grieving queen in great detail, and Catherine began to feel a little contrite for running away so suddenly.

"It seems that she truly believes I have been taken forcefully. Maybe I should send her a message explaining that I'm safe and that I left willfully. If nothing else it might put her mind at ease."

"We can't risk it. The courier would be forced to explain how he received the message, and Humphrey would learn that we are near Strathwick," reasoned Raoul.

"We must free Ossian as soon as possible," interrupted Jacob, feeling responsible for his imprisonment in those horrible dungeons. He pictured his friend's face slowly transforming into the ghost-like countenances of the other prisoners.

"I know you would like to storm the castle right now, Jacob, but getting yourself killed or captured won't do Ossian any good. The only way we can help him now is by finishing this task," replied Raoul.

"I'm worried about two things," said the former queen. She was breathing normally now, and her cheeks had returned to their usual color. "First of all, there are guards traveling all throughout the kingdom as we speak. Even as we stand here we risk being discovered. Secondly, they are posting a drawing of Jacob wherever they go. We'll have to be extremely cautious as we travel in order to avoid being captured."

"Let's be off then without delay." Raoul quickly strode over to his horse. "Jacob will ride Mabel alone, and Elizabeth and Catherine will have to travel on the black mare together. We'll try and find another horse as soon as possible."

After mounting his horse he added, "There are still a few hours of daylight remaining, and I think we should try and distance ourselves as far from Strathwick as possible before we stop for the night. We'll eat when we find a place that is safe enough to make a shelter and start a fire for cooking." It was obvious to the others that Raoul was determined to leave quickly, so without arguing they mounted their assigned horses and followed behind him as he sped away to the west. After a few hundred yards, the small band of riders veered slightly to the south and encountered the dirt road that led away from Strathwick. Jacob, looking back over his shoulder occasionally, watched as the city grew smaller and smaller behind him.

Someday, he thought. *Someday.*

A few more hours passed by without any excitement.

Catherine had been hoping for something a little more interesting than just an endless dirt road, an empty stomach, and a very sore buttocks. "I just realized that we have at least three more days of travel before we reach Woodhurst, and even then we will only have gained the second figurine," she complained loudly to Elizabeth, her riding companion. It was obvious that she had already become tired of the routine.

Elizabeth smiled. "Don't worry. I doubt this whole trip will be as boring as you fear it will be, although I hope that I'm wrong."

Raoul, who was riding ahead of the others, slowed his horse to a walk and allowed them to catch up. When they did, he said, "It's nearly sunset now, and we need to find a place to sleep for the night. This is a well-traveled road, and there should be plenty of suitable locations if we aren't too particular."

"There are many thieves and burglars who sneak around these busy roads," warned Elizabeth. "It would still be wise to find a hidden location."

"Thieves?" questioned Jacob. "How do they dare steal and rob others when they know about Humphrey's tyrannical laws and consequences?"

"It's Humphrey's laws that have created this problem," Elizabeth answered. "Many good men have been forced to turn to thievery in order to provide for their families. The taxes imposed upon them are much too high. It has become a very serious problem throughout much of the kingdom."

As Raoul led them quietly toward a small thicket of trees, Jacob was deep in thought. His life at the castle had always been difficult and full of toil, but he had never gone hungry and was always well clothed. He had slept comfortably in a soft bed and had never been in any real danger. Had his life of comfort contributed to the sufferings and hardships of these people? Would he himself turn to burglary if he needed to keep his friends and family from starvation? He had lived a sheltered life, both physically and mentally, and had not experienced the deprivation and hardships of the people of Avondale.

Someday, I will make a difference! he vowed.

As the weary and sore riders neared the thicket where they would rest for the night, Raoul motioned for the others to be quiet. Slowing his horse to a stop, he dismounted. Jacob did the same.

"We should make sure that no one has already sought refuge here for the night, Jacob. You now have the skill to approach the grove silently," whispered Raoul. "Please be careful."

Jacob's face formed into the widest grin that Raoul had ever seen, and before he could change his mind, the heir of Avondale eerily and silently crept away. The older man led the horses back to where Elizabeth and Catherine were still sitting atop the black mare.

"Now we wait," he said, "and worry."

CHAPTER 26

Jacob was surprised at how noiselessly he could move about the trees and bushes all around him. He was trying intently to avoid stepping on any fallen, dried twigs and branches. Even his fluid motions and quiet breathing came completely natural to him as he stealthily circled the thicket in silence, staying in the shadows. The sun was setting, and the silhouettes of the trees were long and dark as they leaned toward the east. Jacob could see surprisingly well in the low light that was slowly overtaking the thick cover.

Approximately fifteen minutes had passed when Jacob saw that he was nearly finished with his investigation of the small grove. In fact, he was just about to stand up and walk noisily back to where the others were waiting when he heard a faint whisper coming from a few feet to his left. He froze instantly and held his breath.

"Piers, I know I saw 'em comin' toward us. There was three horses en four riders, en they looked like wealthy folk t'me."

"Well, Gerard, if they *were* coming, they would have entered the thicket by now," came a soft reply from Jacob's right. "Next time *I* will be the lookout." Jacob didn't dare exhale. He knew that he was dangerously positioned directly between two men who meant him and his friends harm. They were obviously thieves who were planning to ambush the unsuspecting travelers so they could take their food, their valuables, and maybe even their lives. His lungs felt as if they would explode. Unable to hold his breath any longer, Jacob slowly exhaled as quietly as he could and took in a much-needed breath. He waited again in silence, wondering if he had been heard.

"They must've changed their minds 'bout spendin' the night 'ere. There goes our dinner," sighed the burglar to his left, a little more loudly than before.

"Have a little patience. Someone may still come before too long," hissed his partner. "It is too late for anyone traveling to Strathwick to arrive before the gates are closed. We should wait for a while yet."

Long minutes passed by in silence. Darkness settled in. The cloud-covered half moon looking down from above provided just enough light for Jacob to see the center of the thicket. It was, at most, ten or fifteen yards away and provided enough of a clearing for only a small group of people to rest for the night. Jacob guessed that Piers and Gerard knew the location well and worked here often.

I wonder how well they can see in this darkness, Jacob thought, not knowing how much the lion's abilities had affected his eyesight.

After another minute or two of waiting, Jacob noticed a slight movement on the other side of the small clearing.

Are there three robbers? Jacob wondered.

He saw the movement again, but this time he also heard a slight rustling sound.

"Jou' 'ear that, Piers?" whispered Gerard almost inaudibly.

"Sure did. Get ready."

"We jus' might be eatin' after all."

"Be quiet and wait for my signal. You have your knife ready?"

"Oh, it's ready a'right."

It was obvious to Jacob that whoever was coming was in serious trouble. He knew that if he cried out a warning he would be discovered and attacked within seconds.

"Jacob, where are you?" came the soft voice of Raoul as he stepped cautiously out into the open. "Jacob? Jacob, can you hear me?"

Quickly scanning the sky above, Jacob saw that the moon was still hiding behind a thick white cloud. He knew that the grove must have been quite dark, yet he was surprised at how well he could see his friend standing there in the clearing, holding his own knife out in front of him.

"Now, Gerard!" A loud yell erupted from Jacob's right.

Branches and shrubs snapped loudly as the tall, wiry thief jumped from his hiding place no more than a foot from Jacob's right. Jacob lunged forward and grabbed Piers's ankles with both hands. The surprised criminal let out a resounding yelp as he fell forward. He bounced off a sturdy tree trunk, and struck the solid ground awkwardly. He lay there unconscious.

Upon hearing Piers's signal, Gerard had left his position and was now lumbering straight toward Raoul as quickly as he could. He was tall like Piers, but Gerard's body was as thick as his mind seemed to be.

"Where is 'e? I can't see 'im!" he yelled as he blindly slashed his sharp knife back and forth as he ran.

Jacob, who was standing directly on top of the already fallen thief, could see that Raoul had become quite disoriented by the darkness and the commotion. Instead of looking in the direction of the galumphing robber, he was spinning around from side to side, expecting to be attacked from any direction at any time. He didn't know that a dangerous knife was rushing toward him.

"Raoul! Look out!" Jacob yelled as he charged forward. He quickly covered the short distance between himself and the robber.

Jacob dove hard into the man's side. A loud crunching sound came from the thief's ribcage, and he groaned in pain as he fell to the earth. Unfazed by the blow, Jacob rolled quickly to his feet, unsheathed his powerful sword, and held it high above his head. Instantly the grove was completely filled with an intense white light as bright as the noon-day sun. It poured out from the ancient weapon. Jacob stood there majestically, ready to strike.

As the magical blade shone brilliantly from above Jacob's head, it illuminated the terror-stricken face of his new captive. The frightened man, blinded by the powerful light, closed his eyes tightly and waited for the fatal blow that would end his life. It never came.

Jacob slowly lowered the wondrous sword to his side. As he did so, the brightness of the blade gradually faded to a shimmer, and the receding light abandoned the tops of the tall trees, traveled slowly down their long slender trunks, and eventually settled into the center of the clearing where Jacob stood.

"Where 'jou come from?" asked Gerard, who had opened his eyes. "And 'ou are you?" He stared in awe at the glowing blade and then looked nervously at its bearer's eyes.

Raoul, standing next to Jacob, said, "I would like to know the same thing. Where *did* you come from?"

Turning toward Raoul, Jacob beheld a mixed look of astonishment and pride on his friend's face. "I'll tell you later, but for now we had better go get Piers."

"You know their names?"

"It's a long story," Jacob replied with a smile.

As the six of them, two bound with thick rope, sat around the small fire in the center of the grove, Jacob explained what had happened. He was careful to leave out any mention of his inhuman abilities as he gave his version of the encounter with Piers and Gerard. He wasn't sure how he could hide the fact that his sword was special. Gerard had seen it.

As he arrived at the part in the story when he unsheathed his sword and raised it above his head, Jacob simply left out the fact that the blade had emitted a blinding white light.

Gerard, as thick-skulled as he first appeared, seemed to catch on. His eyes met Jacob's, and they exchanged a silent understanding.

Raoul, Elizabeth, and Catherine also remained quiet about the magical broadsword.

After Jacob finished his account, there were a few minutes of silence. Only the crackling of the fire and the sound of crickets chirping in the darkness could be heard.

Piers, who seemed to be quietly contemplating his part in the failed robbery, simply sat there with a bandaged gash on his bony forehead.

Elizabeth finally broke the silence. "You two are lucky that you tried to rob such compassionate people, you know. It's likely that anyone else would have killed you without hesitation."

"Yes, ma'am. I'm dun with thiev'ry now. I nev'r did like it much," answered Gerard as he twisted his shoulders back and forth, wondering how his side could hurt so badly.

"Well, if that's a promise, I will ask my husband to untie you."

"Yes, ma'am, as I a'ready said, I am dun. That's a promise."

"You too, Piers if you promise."

"I don't know how else I will eat, but I guess I'll promise too." Piers frowned.

"Are you sure about this, Elizabeth?" questioned Raoul. "Just a short time ago these men were armed with knives and were intent on robbing us. What do we do with them now?"

The answer on his wife's face caused him to lean over and untie the binding ropes.

"I'll buy their knives from them," she proposed. "You have already taken them anyway. They will have the money they need, and we will keep their weapons." She stood and walked over to her mare, and when she returned she was holding two gold coins and a small sack of dried fruits and meats.

The newly reformed criminals' eyes went wide with wonder as the kind woman handed each of them a golden coin and a handful of food.

As she passed the sack around to the rest of the famished group, Elizabeth said, "It looks like we won't be hunting for supper tonight, so eat up."

Soon the bag of food was empty.

Raoul stood up. "It looks like a nice enough evening to sleep under the stars. I'll stand watch for a few hours, and then I'll wake Jacob. The two of us will alternate sleep until morning." After retrieving blankets from the packs on the horses, he handed them out to everyone around.

When they were all situated as comfortably as possible, he looked directly at Piers and said, "We will part ways in the morning, and you will not speak to anyone about the events of tonight. You never met us."

The wiry man nodded his head in agreement. "Believe me, sir, I have no desire to tell anyone about this night. It paints me as a fool and a beggar."

"Better a beggar than a thief," Raoul answered under his breath as he walked away to stand guard over the others. It would be a long night.

CHAPTER 27

Jacob awoke in the morning to a delicious aroma lingering in the air. He and Raoul had each taken their turns watching over the company throughout the night, but even when it was his time to sleep Jacob found it difficult. The ground was hard and uneven, and the thin blanket did little to fight off the cold nighttime air. Now he felt sore all over, and he was hungry.

Sitting upright and looking toward the fire, Jacob saw that Raoul was roasting something on a spit. "You have been hunting," Jacob pointed out.

"Sure have."

"What's for breakfast?"

"Roasted hare and fresh berries. Four hares, actually. Got them with my crossbow."

The conversation between Jacob and Raoul stirred the others from their slumber.

"Sounds delicious," said Catherine as she rolled over, slowly stood up, and began shaking her blanket aggressively.

"The food seems to be ready, and we have a long day ahead of us, so let's eat," replied the weary chef. "Drink all of the water you would like. I found a small stream not far from here where we can refill our bottles and replenish the horses."

Unlike the meager supper from the night before, there was plenty of food to go around, and everyone ate and drank until their bellies were full.

After the fire was extinguished, the packs were organized, and before long Jacob and his party were sitting atop their horses and speaking their good-byes to Piers and Gerard.

"Remember what I said," reminded Raoul sternly.

"Yessir," answered the two men, nearly simultaneously.

"And your promise," said Elizabeth.

"Yes, ma'am," said Gerard, who then gave Piers a sharp jab to his side when he noticed that the thin man hadn't replied.

"Yes, ma'am," Piers said quietly.

Raoul led the way again as he turned and galloped to the stream, and it wasn't long before the horses' stomachs and the leather bottles were filled and ready for the long ride ahead.

"Get on your horses. We have some long days ahead," Raoul announced.

"There it is. That's Woodhurst," said Raoul as he and the others glanced down at the settlement from the top of a small, tree-covered hill.

They had left the road a few miles back in order to approach the village cautiously from the north. The ever-careful Raoul didn't want to risk being seen by anyone.

"I've never been so excited to see anything in my entire life," said Catherine as she slid off the saddle from behind Elizabeth and landed wobbly-legged onto the soft, grassy earth.

The others followed her lead and dismounted their horses. Raoul skillfully tied up the three hungry and weary animals, which began grazing eagerly.

"No offense, Elizabeth, but we have got to get another horse." Catherine stretched her sore muscles.

"I think my mare would agree," replied Elizabeth with a smile. "We should be able to purchase one here in Woodhurst."

"We were lucky to avoid being recognized during our journey here, but we should still be cautious," Raoul reminded them. "It's likely that some of the royal guards have already arrived and have posted notices in the village. In fact, they might even still be here, so it would be a good idea for Jacob and Catherine to avoid going into Woodhurst at all."

"It would," remarked Jacob, not the least bit surprised.

"Where will we stay?" questioned Catherine. "We don't know how long we will be here as we look for the hawk figurine, and I surely wouldn't complain about a soft bed and a genuine meal or two." The recent days had been filled with long rides, restless nights, and little food.

Raoul smiled. "Nor would I. Adventures are not as enjoyable as they might first appear, now are they?"

"It's a secluded place to live though, isn't it?" interrupted Jacob as he intently studied the small village before him.

Woodhurst was not only much smaller in size than was Strathwick, but, as its name implied, all of the houses and buildings were made entirely out of wood.

"It's not as tucked away as *I* would prefer." Raoul laughed as he strolled over and stood next to Jacob. "But I have been accused of being a bit of a recluse, you know."

"Can you believe the size of those trees?" questioned Jacob as his attention turned to Woodhurst's outer fortification. "Somehow the villagers have placed those massive tree trunks together to form a wall. I would have never imagined that trees could grow so large."

Catherine, who had been too busy working out her knotted muscles to focus her attention on the village, came over and stood at Jacob's left. "Those trunks must be a hundred and fifty feet long and fifteen feet wide, or fifteen feet tall, I guess I should say, now that they are lying on their sides! How did they ever cut them down and move them here?"

Jacob's mind had just turned to his next task. As he pictured one of those tree trunks standing straight up and disappearing into the sky, his stomach lurched.

"People can do amazing things when they set their minds to it," answered Elizabeth. She was speaking of the villagers' amazing feat of creating the wooden wall, but her words comforted Jacob even so.

"I don't see any trees that large around here." Raoul glanced at the woods around him and at the thick forest lying west of the village. "They are much too large to have been moved a very long distance. The king of trees can't be very far away."

"Raoul and I will go into Woodhurst and ask about food, lodging, and a horse. If we can, we'll also ask around to see if someone can point us in the direction of a very large tree," Elizabeth suggested. "You two should—"

"Stay here," interrupted Jacob and Catherine at the same time.

"Exactly," replied Elizabeth with a smile. "I believe you two are catching on."

The future king and the former princess watched as Elizabeth and Raoul descended the small hill upon which they were standing, stepped onto the road, and walked the short distance to the wooden gate that served as the entrance to Woodhurst. After speaking for a moment with the posted sentry, the man stepped aside and allowed them passage into the village.

Jacob turned to Catherine and asked, "Are you still glad that you chose to join me in this adventure?"

"I've never been so sore, hungry, or tired in my entire life."

"It *has* been a lot more exhausting and a little less exciting than expected." Jacob had hoped for a different answer, and his face betrayed him.

"Jacob, you know that I would make the very same decision again without hesitation."

His countenance brightened slightly. "Well, I can't help with the sore and tired, but the hungry might be something that I can make right. Wait here." He slipped into the woods to look for some dinner.

"Gladly," Catherine replied under her breath as she found a large, moss-covered rock to sit on and lean against. The moist, grassy earth felt like a feather mattress compared to the old leather saddle that she had been sitting in for the last many days. Leaning back to rest her head on the mossy boulder, Catherine closed her eyes and tilted her head upward to allow the warmth of the sun to soothe her face and mind. Moments later she was asleep.

CHAPTER 28

"Heee-a! Heee-a!" came a high-pitched shrill, loud enough to jolt Catherine from her sleep. She opened her eyes just in time to see an enormous goshawk diving directly toward her, its sharp talons just yards away and ready to pierce their prey. Catherine screamed as she instinctively rolled to her right. The massive bird screeched again and corrected its course. Catherine dove headlong into the thick brush behind the mossy boulder. Her heart beat quickly and she gasped for air. She lay flat on her side, quickly pulling her knees into her chest, wrapping her arms around her legs. "Jacob!" she called frantically at the top of her voice.

Huge wings blocked the sunlight above, creating an ominous shadow as the hawk continued to plummet downward. Catherine was defenseless. She silently pleaded with the thick cover to protect her.

"Heee-a!"

Catherine peered through the branches above her and watched the goshawk flair its wings and sweep just inches above the brush that shielded her. A rush of wind and a pungent odor passed over her as the enormous raptor yawed to its left and began ascending into the sky above.

Catherine lay there and waited while her heartbeat returned to normal, watching the hawk slowly fly skyward.

It must have a wingspan of seven or eight feet! she thought. She nervously rose to her feet and weaved her way out of the brush. Standing in the small clearing, in front of the large boulder, Catherine brushed the dirt, twigs, and leaves from her clothing. Her bare arms were scratched and bleeding, but she was alive. Her hands were shaking. There was no doubt in Catherine's mind that this was the hawk that would lead them to the next figurine. "Jacob, come quickly!" she yelled as loudly as she could. "Hurry, Jacob!"

As she waited for Jacob to return, Catherine continued to watch the majestic raptor as its powerful wings carried it through the midday sky. It would climb high enough to become just a dot in the heavens, and then it would dive swiftly toward the earth while screaming its piercing call. Just before reaching the tree tops, the goshawk would spread its powerful wings and end its rapid descent by completing a graceful arc.

The hawk repeated this process of climbing and diving over and over again as it flew farther and farther away from where Catherine stood. At last the monstrous bird climbed one final time, higher than ever before, screeched its ear-splitting cry, and dove straight into the forest at full speed, just a mile or so beyond the village. It didn't emerge again.

"Jacob!" yelled Catherine excitedly, turning around and facing the woods that Jacob had entered earlier. "Where are you?" Catherine's fear was gone.

"I'm coming, Catherine. Almost there!" came Jacob's faint reply.

Seconds later he was emerging from the woods, moving very quickly. His sword was drawn and glowing brightly as he rushed to Catherine's aid. He stopped abruptly at her side and quickly glanced all around him, alert and ready for battle and panting heavily.

"Are you okay? Why did you scream?"

"I found the winged beast! Well, *it* found *me* I guess. It tried to attack me." Catherine showed Jacob the scratches on her arms. Jacob's eyes grew wide, and then his face formed an angry scowl. Catherine laughed. "These are from the branches over there, not the talons. I wouldn't be here at all had that goshawk gotten a hold of me. Anyway, I know where to look for the figurine— sort of."

Jacob's face softened as his worry and anger faded. "I shouldn't have left you here alone."

"You didn't know that would happen. Besides, it's about time there was some excitement around here."

Catherine explained everything that had happened since Jacob had left to go hunting. She described the goshawk's actions in great detail and pointed at the location on the horizon where it had plunged into the forest.

"I think you're right," Jacob answered when she ended her story. "There can be only one hawk that large in all of Avondale. It *must* be the hawk whose nest we are looking for. We need to act quickly."

"What about Raoul and Elizabeth?" questioned Catherine. "Shouldn't we wait for them?"

"It isn't safe to go into the village to find them, and we don't even know how long they'll be gone. I think we should go and find the nest, get the figurine, and return quickly before night settles in. We can leave them a message so they don't worry."

"I don't think that will keep them from worrying, but I do agree that we should try and find the hawk as soon as possible."

Catherine located parchment and ink from Raoul's horse-pack and scribed a quick message explaining that they had seen the hawk and would be back before nightfall. Jacob untied Mabel and readied her for their quick trip into the forest. He also made sure that they had a small supply of food and water.

"Okay. Which way do we go?" asked Jacob after the two of them were ready and sitting atop Mabel's back.

"Well, the hawk disappeared into the forest about a mile or so beyond the village just to the right of that tower there," Catherine pointed to a tall lookout at the west end of town.

Jacob studied the location and glanced at the sun's position in the sky. "I think if we get close enough we will know the tree when we see it. Now we just need to get around Woodhurst without being seen."

Urging Mabel down the hill and around the northwest part of the village, Jacob made sure to stay just inside the line of trees. It was fairly slow going, but before too long they were on the other side of the village and looking back at the hill where they had been hiding minutes earlier.

"Based on where you last saw the hawk, I think this is about right," said Jacob as he pulled on Mabel's reins, urging her to a stop. After dismounting the mare and helping Catherine down from the saddle, he said, "You follow the tree line in that direction and see if you can find a trailhead. I'll search over here."

It wasn't more than a minute or two when Catherine called out, "Jacob, over here! I found one!"

Jacob quickly rushed over to where Catherine was standing. "Is that a trail or a road?" he asked. "It must be twenty-five feet wide, and it is perfectly straight for as far as I can see."

"It seems to be going in the right direction," Catherine said excitedly. "This might be easier than we thought."

"I guess we'll find out," Jacob replied as he jumped back onto Mabel's saddle and pulled Catherine up behind him. He tapped his feet into the large mare's sides. "Okay, Mabel, take us to the king of trees."

As Jacob and Catherine galloped down the wide trail they hoped would lead them to the next figurine, they were quiet. Jacob was thinking about the incredible amount of labor that had been required to clear away so many trees from the dense forest around them. This impressive manmade pathway was wide enough to qualify as a road but felt more like a trail, since it was covered with grass, wildflowers, and fallen leaves and twigs.

Perhaps more impressive than the perfect straightness and obvious width of the trail was the fact that not even a single stump was slightly visible above the earth anywhere along the way. Every thirty or forty feet there was a stout log half-buried in the earth running perpendicularly across the trail. These logs had been denuded of bark and were round and smooth except for the last few feet on each end. Luckily, Mabel's long legs allowed her to gallop over the strategically placed logs effortlessly as she carried her curious masters deeper and deeper into the forest.

"We *must* be headed in the right direction, Catherine. The villagers created this trail to drag those massive tree trunks back to Woodhurst. They probably used all of the normal-sized trees that they cut down along the way to build the rest of their buildings."

"I've been thinking the same thing. They must have used horses or oxen to help drag the trees back to the village. Look, it can't be much farther now. The path seems to just disappear up ahead."

"If we are nearly there, why haven't we seen the tree by now, rising up above the others?"

Mabel galloped on, and Jacob and Catherine began to realize why they hadn't yet spotted the tree. They were quickly approaching some sort of basin or valley up ahead. Jacob recognized the sound of a babbling stream that was growing louder with each stride of Mabel's long legs.

"The tree must be down below," Catherine explained. "That's why we weren't able to see it from the village."

Moments later, Jacob and Catherine reached a ridge line, and Jacob pulled back on the reins. The view before them was awe inspiring. The wide manmade pathway transformed into a foot trail that zigzagged down a steep slope into a lush green basin. Not far from the center of the narrow, deep valley, maybe a hundred yards away, was Avondale's king of trees.

There was no question. The tree was at least three hundred and fifty feet tall and nearly fifty feet in diameter at its base. Even though Jacob and Catherine were standing well above the base of the tree that began down in the deepest part of the valley beneath them, they still tipped their heads back slightly to peer up at the top of the mighty tree.

"There's the nest!" yelled Catherine excitedly while pointing at a huge bundle of twigs and branches with her finger. She couldn't see if the goshawk was occupying its roost or not. She hoped not, for Jacob's sake.

"I see it too, Catherine, way up at the top," replied Jacob softly. "Although I wish I hadn't," he added before sliding down from the saddle. Reaching up, he helped Catherine down also.

Hoping to take his mind off of the tree, Jacob walked closer to the ledge in front of him so he could look down and survey the surrounding area. All around the base of the massive tree Jacob saw the stumps of the previously harvested giants. None were even nearly as large as the king before him, but they had been huge trees nonetheless.

"Catherine, they have cut down *all* of the others."

"It's a shame, isn't it?"

"And they would have chopped down that one too if they could have," came a startling reply from behind Catherine, who nearly fell over from fright.

Jacob drew his sword and spun around to see who was behind them.

Laughing loudly after seeing that he had accomplished his goal, Raoul said, "That's what you get for leaving before we could return."

"Well, you didn't expect us to sit there waiting all day, did you? Besides, the hawk showed me exactly where to go." Catherine's face was red and betrayed her emotions.

"I am sorry," replied Raoul, still smiling broadly.

"Where's Elizabeth?" questioned Jacob as he sheathed his sword. He looked down the trail behind Raoul and only saw one horse tethered to a tree a dozen yards away.

"We were told where to find the tree when we asked around the village. After seeing the message that you left behind, we realized that we would probably not be staying in Woodhurst for long. I came to find you while she went in search of a horse for Catherine."

"What did you mean when you said that the villagers would have cut down this tree if they *could* have?" Catherine asked.

"The gentleman who pointed us in this direction warned us that a very large hawk nests in the tree and won't let anyone near it. Apparently some villagers have been severely wounded while trying over the years."

"That's just great!" replied Jacob, who was already nervous about climbing the tree. "Not only do I have to climb to the top of that giant, but now I have to avoid being torn to shreds by a sharp beak and skin-piercing talons."

Jacob tethered Mabel to a nearby tree and began descending the foot trail that led to the valley floor. Raoul and Catherine shadowed behind. As he followed the winding path beneath his feet, Jacob looked around at the wondrous world around him. A crystal-clear brook twisted and turned along the valley floor as it flowed from the north to the south, dividing sections of green grass and flowers and other vegetation. The hill on other side of the valley was actually the base of the mountain range that the people of Avondale had always considered to be the western border of their kingdom. These rolling foothills sloped away gently for a number of miles before jutting nearly straight upward into the tall, snow-covered peaks above.

The steepness of the winding trail, and perhaps the frightening task that he would soon be facing, caused Jacob to descend slowly to the valley below. Eventually he and the others were standing at the edge of the basin and staring at the enormous tree some thirty or forty yards to the west.

While planning his strategy for climbing the towering tree, Jacob noticed that the lowest branch was at least forty-five feet from the ground, and the trunk was much too wide to wrap his arms and legs around.

"How am I supposed to even get started?"

Raoul answered, "The bark may be coarse and knobby enough to get you up to the level of the branches. I don't see any other way."

"Look!" yelled Catherine as she pointed upward nervously. "It's the hawk!"

Jacob and Raoul looked up to see the goshawk quietly and slowly circling the tree as it descended from its nest high above. With each circle the majestic raptor came nearer, and its huge size became more and more evident. The undersides of its broad wings and long tail were a barred brown and grey, and it wore a horizontal white stripe above each eye that made it seem as if it was scowling at the new intruders.

Upon approaching the bottom branch of the tree, the intimidating hawk flared out is powerful wings, spread its tail wide, and gracefully landed on the thick limb. It seemed to be purposely displaying its long, sharp talons as its feet wrapped around the branch upon which it perched. The goshawk then quietly stared its piercing eyes directly at Jacob and the others.

"You're right, Catherine. That thing would have carried you away."

"It's both frightening and majestic, isn't it?" Feeling much safer with Jacob and Raoul by her side, Catherine said, "Let's see what she does." She took a small, deliberate step toward the trunk of the tree.

"Heee-a!" shrieked the hawk menacingly while spreading its wings out wide, ready to take flight.

Catherine stepped quickly backward, and the bird slowly tucked its wings back into its body and became quiet again. It resumed its scowling gaze.

"First of all, Catherine, all you did was upset the thing, and secondly, why did you call it a she?" questioned Jacob.

"Any bird that is that protective of its nest has to be female," reasoned Catherine. "And I wanted to see what she would do if you tried to climb the tree. Now we know."

"I'll try and distract her while you hurry to the tree's base," offered Raoul. "We are going to be running out of daylight in a couple of hours. There is no time to waste."

Raoul ran briefly toward the tree and then darted to his left in an attempt to draw the hawk away. While shrieking another warning, the goshawk dove instantly from the branch, and with her wings spread wide and her knife-like talons jutting out beneath her, plunged rapidly toward the fleeing man.

It only took a few seconds for the hawk to cover the distance between her perch and Raoul. Realizing that he was in serious danger, Raoul threw himself to the earth in an attempt to get away, lying as flat on his stomach as he possibly could. The diving goshawk's sharp talons narrowly missed him. She shrieked again as she flew upward and prepared for another attack. Quickly scrambling to his feet, Raoul rushed back to Jacob's side and stood there absolutely still—he didn't dare move even a single muscle.

"Well, that didn't work, did it?" he said breathlessly.

The winged protector simply circled around gracefully and flew back over to the tree, resuming her position on the sturdy branch.

Jacob was at a total loss. He knew that he needed to climb the tree, but it seemed impossible. His only hope was that his lion abilities would help him evade the hawk while he stormed the tree.

"Okay, if I can just make it up to the first branches I should be all right," Jacob reasoned. "I'll stay near the center of the tree as I climb, and the dense limbs will protect me."

Jacob removed the scabbard at his side, with the sword still sheathed inside, and handed it to Catherine.

"Here goes!" he said as he started walking briskly toward the tree while keeping his eyes on the goshawk.

Every muscle in his body was tense and ready to react to whatever move the raptor made.

The goshawk leapt from the branch, tucked her wings into her side, and dove straight towards Jacob.

Jacob began to run.

CHAPTER 29

Just seconds after launching from her perch, the fierce hawk was closing in on Jacob. She spread her wings out and jutted her feet forward, ready to grasp him by the shoulders.

Jacob dove into a roll, narrowly avoiding the dangerous claws. He scrambled to his right and picked up a jagged rock. The goshawk turned around to attack again, shrieking loudly as she hurtled downward. Jacob threw the rock as hard as he could. The bird veered sharply and the stone whizzed by, narrowly missing its intended target. The hawk flipped gracefully in the air and plummeted toward Jacob again.

Jacob sprinted straight toward the hawk. As he ran, he reached down with his right hand, grasped a sturdy broken branch from the ground, and jumped onto a wide tree stump in front of him.

The goshawk continued her assault, diving directly at her new enemy. She prepared herself for battle, talons ready and wings half tucked.

Jacob took two long strides across the top of the tree stump and leapt into the air. He twisted his body sideways and swung the branch as hard as he could. The wooden limb snapped in two as it struck the right wing of the massive bird.

The hawk screeched in pain, pulled her injured wing into her side, and tumbled to the ground, hitting the earth with a soft thump.

Jacob landed skillfully on both feet, and dropped the piece of branch he was still holding.

"I didn't want to hurt you!" Jacob yelled.

The hawk rose to her feet and tested her sore wing by spreading it as widely as she could. After glaring at Jacob one more time, she ran and took to the air, flying awkwardly away, staying close to the ground. She landed on a branch in a small tree about thirty yards away, and fluttered her right wing again.

Jacob was still trembling slightly as he looked back at Catherine and Raoul. They must have felt safer where they were standing at the base of the trail, because they hadn't moved an inch during the entire fight .

Remembering his task Jacob walked to the base of the towering giant. He tilted his head back to take in the full stature of the monstrous tree before him. Even the coarse bark seemed to stand at attention, daring him to step any closer to the mighty fortress.

Okay then, here I go!

After finding his first good foothold with his right foot, Jacob pushed off with his left and began to climb Avondale's king of trees.

Even with his inhuman abilities, it took Jacob nearly twenty minutes to climb the lofty tree that held the hawk figurine. He had been careful to never look down along the way and had tried to stay focused on the branch just above him the entire time. As he had climbed steadily up the towering giant, its branches and limbs had grown thinner and shorter, and its trunk diameter had tapered down to the point that it nearly equaled the width of an average tree trunk.

"I should be near the nest now," said Jacob as he glanced all around while sitting near the top of the evergreen. Looking upward and toward what he guessed was the east side of the tree, Jacob could barely discern the shape of the nest through the dense branches and thick needles.

Excited that he had found it, Jacob quickly climbed for another minute or so until he could see the nest more clearly. It was the biggest nest that he had ever seen, and it was positioned dangerously out on a limb about six feet away from the trunk of the tree.

Jacob wondered if it was possible that the goshawk could have lived all of these years. It was almost unimaginable, but nothing else that had happened to him during the last week seemed possible either.

After scooting himself across the branch and over to the large, old nest, Jacob recited the memorized inscription from the sword.

Seek the winged beast that doth ride the breeze,

And nests on Avondale's king of trees.

Look beneath the roost, the hawk to obtain,

And sight, not flight, ye then will gain.

Leaning over into the wide nest, Jacob reached his hand into its center. The top layer was soft and lined with feathers, grass, and leaves. As he gently pushed his hand farther into the nest, he felt it, a small metal object that was just the right size. Pulling it out carefully so as to not drop it and lose it forever, Jacob held the golden figurine to admire it. Its wings were outstretched, and its sharp talons looked as if they were grasping something.

Carefully, Jacob removed the silk pouch from around his neck and placed the figurine inside. After tightening the drawstring, he repositioned the pouch over his head and beneath his shirt.

Well, once again, I don't feel any differently, Jacob thought. What he did feel was a profound sense of accomplishment.

"Heeeeeeeee-a!" came the goshawk's call from the sky above.

Looking up, Jacob watched as she circled, struggling only slightly with her sore right wing. He was happy to see that she would be okay. As he focused on the flight of the hawk, his head began to spin, and an acute dizziness overcame him, causing him to shut his eyes tightly. After a brief moment, the lightheadedness left, and when Jacob opened his eyes again his vision was extraordinarily clear, and the hawk that was so far away just seconds before suddenly zoomed into view.

It seemed to Jacob that she was just a few feet away. Then, just as suddenly as it came, Jacob's hawk vision left, and the large raptor zoomed back out until she was just a dot on the horizon. Jacob's head spun, and he felt as if he was going to fall. He scrambled over to the trunk of the tree and grasped it tightly while closing his eyes and waiting for the spinning to stop.

It's a good thing I haven't had much to eat today, Jacob thought as his stomach churned angrily.

After a minute or two he opened his eyes and began slowly descending the tree. It took longer than the climb had taken, because he was still feeling slightly dizzy, but less than thirty minutes later Jacob was approaching the tree's lowest branch. Wanting to test his new ability, he sat on the bottom branch where the hawk had been perched earlier and looked over at Raoul and Catherine. It seemed they were still too frightened to approach the tree.

Jacob waved to them and smiled as he looked at the valley around him. His vision was definitely clearer than before. The details of the trees and flowers were sharper and possibly even more colorful. He could detect flashes of movements of insects and small animals in the fields around him. Jacob heard Catherine yell something but couldn't tell what she had said. He looked in her direction as she yelled again. Still he couldn't hear the individual words. As he focused on her face intently, his head spun again, yet less severely than before, and his sight zoomed in until he could see nothing more than her soft red lips. As she yelled again this time, he could see what she was saying.

"Did…you…get…it?"

Jacob's vision zoomed back out, and he once again closed his eyes to steady himself. After a few seconds he was able to begin his descent down the knobby trunk to the soft earth below. As his feet touched the ground, he felt a surge of relief and appreciation rush over him. He turned and ran to the others.

"We were worried about you," said Raoul. "You were gone for nearly an hour."

Jacob removed the golden figurine from his pouch. "I was worried about myself also," he said with a smile. "And by the way, this vision thing is going to require some practice."

Jacob took the sword from Catherine and removed it from its scabbard. The brilliant blade and beautiful gem shone brightly. Turning the sword over to the side with the coat of arms, Jacob carefully aligned the figurine with its place in the carving on the blade. Just as the lion did before, the hawk figurine fused with the sword, and the piercing scream of a goshawk echoed through the valley.

"Three to go," said Jacob loudly, his ears ringing.

Catherine and Raoul, who had expected the high-pitched shriek, uncovered their ears and looked intently at the sword, waiting for the inscription to appear. Seconds later it did.

Go to where the waters join and stand atop the polished stone.

A northward gaze reveals a clue that none can see but you alone.

Focus well to see the crag and on it find the piscine cave.

It can't be seen without the sight the little golden raptor gave.

Jacob and the others took turns reading the clue until all were confident that they could remember it well. He then sheathed the sword and said, "It's nearly time for sleep and well past time for food. Should we go?"

"We should meet Elizabeth as soon as we can. She'll be worried about us," replied Raoul.

What's taking them so long? wondered the former queen of Avondale. Elizabeth was pacing back and forth. She had returned from buying a horse for Catherine, a strong, light-brown stallion named Oswyn. To keep her mind occupied, she had set up a small camp a little farther into the forest than before, laid out the bedding for the night, and prepared a meager dinner for everyone. When she could think of nothing else to do, she began pacing. The others arrived just before nightfall.

Elizabeth was excited to hear the account of how Jacob climbed the tree and retrieve the hawk figurine, but was disappointed that she wasn't able to see the majestic bird.

Jacob promised to return with her after completing their quest, and that seemed to appease her. The conversation ended, eyelids grew heavy, and as was customary, Jacob and Raoul took turns standing watch for the night.

"Good morning, Jacob." Raoul sat up from the hard ground and looked in the direction of the crackling fire.

"Good morning to you. Would you like some boar on a stick for breakfast?"

"Sounds surprisingly delicious." Raoul wandered over, sat near the fire, and took the skewered pig from Jacob's outstretched arms. "You're becoming quite the hunter."

"Last night's supper of dried meats and fruits left me hungry. Besides, I wanted to test the goshawk's keen vision together with the lion's stealth this morning." Jacob took a large bite of the roasted wild boar.

"It's *your* keen vision and *your* stealth and agility that made for a successful hunt. And the other skills that you will obtain will certainly be useful for you as you try to regain the throne. However, it is your innate kindness, loyalty, and bravery that will serve you best throughout your life. You were chosen for this task because of who you are, not because of what you will become."

"Well spoken, Raoul," said Elizabeth, who had been awakened by the conversation between her husband and son.

She too wandered over to the fire and took a seat on the fallen log, squeezing in between the two men. Catherine remained fast asleep.

"To Aberfield, then?" questioned Elizabeth. "That is where the Kelbeck and the Upper Stanbourne merge."

"I think so," answered Raoul. "There must be a large boulder or rock that Jacob is supposed to stand on."

"I thought about it during the night," Jacob said. "I'll use the hawk's vision to search the northern mountains for a cave. The figurine will probably be inside."

"Not just any cave. A piscine cave. The Latin word *piscis* means fish," Elizabeth explained.

"I thought we were done with Latin," mumbled Catherine as she rolled over and sat up from her sleep. Her tangled hair was sticking out in all directions, and there was a fallen leaf stuck to her right cheek.

Jacob, Raoul, and Elizabeth laughed impolitely.

"I'm sure I don't look any worse off than the three of you." Catherine smiled as she rubbed her tired and swollen eyes.

"Somehow you pull it off quite well, Catherine," Jacob replied, grinning. "Although it wouldn't hurt to go into Woodhurst and buy yourself a mirror," he added teasingly.

Catherine, reaching over to the ground next to her bedding, found a small stick and hurled it in Jacob's direction. It hit him square in the chest. Catherine joined in on the laughter this time.

"Good aim, Catherine, but next time he says something like that, use a rock," Elizabeth said with a smile as she motioned Catherine over to join the group.

Jacob slid over on the log slightly, allowing Catherine to sit between himself and his mother, who began skillfully working her fingers through the former princess's hair.

"There won't be any fish inside the cave," said Raoul .

"I wouldn't think so," answered Elizabeth. "But even if there were, it still wouldn't be the most peculiar thing to have happened on this adventure."

"By peculiar do you mean things like amazing magical abilities, a giant bird that is hundreds of years old, and Catherine's morning hair?" questioned Jacob with a wide smile.

Catherine reached over and punched Jacob's shoulder. When his eyes met hers, she smiled.

Can eyes smile? wondered Jacob. He was certain that if they could Catherine's were. Jacob had seen this smile many times before and had often wondered if it meant anything. This time he felt certain that it did.

"Well, we may not know why it is called the fish cave until we get there," said Raoul, breaking the silence and causing Jacob and Catherine to return to the conversation.

"Then let's get there quickly." Jacob stood up and began packing up camp.

"The sooner the better." Elizabeth rose to her feet as well.

"I still haven't eaten," said Catherine as she reached for the skewer and took a big bite of boar. "It needs salt or something," she added with a muffled voice while covering her mouth politely. "I wish William was here."

"Hey, I know more about smelling shoes and sweeping floors than preparing breakfast," Jacob replied while shrugging his shoulders.

CHAPTER 30

After riding quickly for nearly two whole days, Jacob and the others had reached the outskirts of Aberfield and set up camp for the night. They had stayed on the road for the most part and had only seen one other group of travelers as they crossed the Beckford Bridge. Jacob guessed they were merchants who were on their way to the markets of Strathwick. They seemed as nervous and worried about seeing other travelers as Raoul did. "I hope Piers and Gerard keep their promise and leave that group alone," Elizabeth had whispered after passing by the small band.

"I believe Gerard has truly changed, but Piers I am not so sure about," Catherine answered.

Overall, the traveling was becoming easier for each member of Jacob's company. Their bodies were becoming used to the seemingly endless riding, and Jacob's stealthy hunting skills were providing them with all of the food they needed.

Catherine and Elizabeth were glad to each have their own horse for this part of the journey. Oswyn was in good physical condition and young and could run nearly as quickly as Mabel. Just like any other horse in the kingdom, however, he couldn't match her endurance. Mabel was definitely one of a kind and had become quite fond of Jacob. She became stubborn if anyone else tried to ride her.

"Well, there's *another* village that I will not see the inside of," said Jacob as the group surveyed the quaint settlement of Aberfield from their hiding position to the west.

The light of the early morning angled down on the village from the east, casting shadows that reached out and pointed toward Jacob's group as if they were trying to reveal their location.

"I'm afraid so," answered Raoul. "This time I will go alone while the three of you wait here. It won't take long since I really only need to find out whether or not any guards are still in the area. And since we probably shouldn't start a fire for cooking, I'll bring back something to eat for breakfast." He mounted his horse and rode away.

Raoul was vigilantly looking out for guards as he rode through the streets of Aberfield searching for food, and more importantly, answers. He suspected that Ambrose wouldn't be in the village since he was likely coordinating the search for Catherine from the royal castle. He knew that he still needed to be careful.

The cobblestone streets seemed to be laid out randomly without any sort of master plan. He found dead ends at nearly every turn, it seemed, and the buildings were in a surprising state of disrepair. *I know I haven't been here for many years now, but I don't remember the village looking so rundown*, Raoul thought as he glanced around at his surroundings.

Seeing a small shop to his left, he dismounted his horse and led him over to a sturdy wooden tethering post. Many years of leather reins had changed the once-rough surface into a smooth, polished timber. Raoul aided in the post's transformation as he looped his own reins around it a few times and tied a loose knot.

Gently patting his horse's side, he whispered, "I won't be long."

He walked over, and opened the creaky door.

The store owner spun around quickly and welcomed Raoul. "What can I do for you today, stranger?" he asked.

"I'm looking for a little food for myself and my traveling companions," answered Raoul.

"As you can see, a *little* food is all that I have," replied the kind man, who smiled at his own joke.

"It appears that times are hard in Aberfield." Raoul gathered some fresh bread and fruit and carried it to the counter. "More difficult even than the rest of the kingdom, it seems."

"The taxes are unbearable for all of us, but here we lack the trade that favors Dalcaster, the large markets of Strathwick, and the forest that provides both food and fuel to the people of Woodhurst. Yes, I suppose we are the poorest people in the kingdom."

Raoul reached into his pocket and retrieved a heavy gold coin. After setting it on the counter, he said, "I would like to buy some information along with this food. I'll give you the coin to keep if it suits you."

"The gold suits me fine," said the wide-eyed shop keep as he stared down at the precious coin. "But I don't have any information *that* valuable."

"That is for me to judge since I am the one asking," replied Raoul kindly. "Are there any royal guards in the village?"

"Yes, sir. But they leave during the day to go searching for a criminal who has escaped the dungeons of the castle. They return at night to question the villagers and demand lodging, food, and drink," answered the man. After pausing briefly, he eyed the gold coin on the counter before him and said, "And they don't pay for any of it."

"And Ambrose, has he been here also?"

"The captain was here briefly a week or so ago, but I haven't seen him since." The shop keep glanced toward the door. "Now, if you please, sir," he said as he handed over the bag of food and motioned toward the door. "Your questions and your gold are making me nervous."

"Thank you." Raoul pushed the coin toward the store owner and left the shop with his bag of food in hand.

He walked down the main road while continuing to survey his surroundings. After turning to his right at the next crossroads, Raoul saw a small group of men and women dressed in worn and tattered clothing, huddled around something that must have caught their collective attention. He slowly approached the group to see what was so interesting. Soon he was close enough to see and hear someone speaking in a loud whisper.

"Ee's a spittn' imudg, I tell ya. I'd know thet face anywhere," said the nearly toothless man as he waved a piece of paper back and forth in front of the untidy crowd. He wouldn't hold it still long enough for Raoul to see what was written on it.

"Can't be," came an answer from one of the men crowded around. "B'sides, it's been 'most twenty years. And 'less you wanna scuffle with the guards whose lookin' for that man, I'd say it's best you keep quiet."

Raoul realized what was happening and took a chance. He normally wasn't one to take chances, but he felt good about this one. "It's not King Rowland. It's his son," he said simply.

The crowd of people turned slowly and focused their attention on the new stranger standing behind them.

After a brief silence the nearly toothless man said, "King Rowland's son? Ya's tellin' us thet this is King Rowland's son?" He held the paper up high with one hand.

"It is," Raoul replied, watching the suspense and wonder build throughout the crowd. Raoul was pleased with the reaction he was getting. He needed that for his plan to work.

"King Rowland didn't have a son," stated a woman from the crowd, who despite having all of her teeth and nicely combed hair, still showed many signs of living in impoverished conditions.

"He did have a son, but you must not tell anyone who has sympathies with the current monarchy." Raoul paused again, waiting for the right time to continue.

The people began to look back and forth at each other in amazement. Raoul leaned in and lowered his voice slightly to increase the sense of mystery. "That is a drawing of Jacob of Avondale, rightful heir to the throne. He will overthrow the kingdom, reign in righteousness, and ease your burdens. He is powerful and strong, equitable and just, and kind and honest."

The crowd clamored excitedly as the people discussed this new information.

"Where is he, then? And what is he waiting for?" asked a man loudly, who was standing to Raoul's right.

Deep silence fell over the group as everyone listened for the answer.

"He was last seen in Dalcaster," answered Raoul. "And he is waiting for each of you."

"For us?" came the question from many in the crowd all at once.

"Whisper it throughout the land. He will need your support. When the timing is right, we will take the castle by storm with Jacob of Avondale riding before us."

The crowd burst into cheers. Hope had been restored. People were hugging and slapping each other on their backs and grinning from ear to ear. Many others came from all around that part of the village to see what the commotion was all about. People whispered frantic messages into the ears of others, who in turn did the same as they began to run down the cobblestone streets looking for someone else to tell.

Raoul smiled and thought, *I hope that was a good idea, because I can't take it back now.*

He quickly retrieved one of the notices still posted on a board behind him and hurried over to his horse. After securing the food in the pack on his horse's back, he folded the paper, stuffed it into his shirt pocket, and headed back to Jacob and the others. The guards were out searching, and he was worried about the safety of his wife and friends.

It didn't seem like very long before Raoul returned with fresh fruit and bread to eat and a concerned look on his face. He sat down near the others and passed out the breakfast, keeping just a little for himself.

"Eat first. We will talk afterward," he said bluntly.

Jacob and the women ate the bread and fruit eagerly, excited to have something to eat that didn't have to be killed, skinned, and roasted on a spit.

When they were finished, Elizabeth was the first to speak. "Okay, dear. What is it?"

"We must leave quickly. Ambrose isn't here, but there are many of his men in the area. They're questioning the villagers at night and searching the whole surrounding region by day. Worse yet, I found this." He withdrew a folded piece of paper from inside his shirt pocket and handed it to Elizabeth.

The former queen unfolded the paper, knowing exactly what she would see but hoping that she was wrong. She held it up to the others. It was one of the notices that had been posted throughout the kingdom. The drawing of Jacob was done quickly but was accurate and skillful.

"They are posted everywhere," said Raoul quietly.

"Well, let's get to where the rivers join quickly and leave this place," suggested Jacob as he jumped to his feet. "We'll travel slowly down the banks of the Kelbeck, staying on the south side of the brook. Raoul and Elizabeth will lead the way, so they can signal us if they see any of the royal guards. We won't be far behind."

Raoul smiled as he too rose to his feet. *He is becoming the man this kingdom needs already*, he thought. *He will be a good king.*

After the four adventurers crossed the brook and began following it downstream to the confluence, Jacob and Catherine paused, allowing Raoul and Elizabeth to gain a lead of a hundred yards or so. Their conversation turned to the next part of their adventure.

"It all seems fairly straightforward except for the part about the fish," said Catherine. "You'll stand on the rock, look northward, and find a cave on or near a rocky cliff."

"I think the cave will be very far away, since it isn't visible to the human eye. I've been trying to practice the hawk vision as often as I can, but it still makes me a little dizzy as the world shifts and whatever I am looking at zooms into view. The best part of my new ability has been the change in my everyday eyesight. Everything is sharper and much clearer than before. ."

Catherine became quiet. She realized that Jacob, her lifelong friend, was becoming Jacob of Avondale. He had a destiny to fulfill. She was certain that he would be a noble, kind, and powerful king. *He knows his path and his purpose. Where will I be when this is all through?* wondered Catherine. She pictured herself wandering the streets of Dalcaster, looking at the faces of every man she saw, wondering if he could be her real father.

The two friends began riding slowly and didn't speak for some time. As they rode, the sounds of the flowing water grew louder and louder.

After a time it was roaring so loudly that Jacob had to raise his voice. "We must be nearly there! Raoul and Elizabeth are probably waiting just up ahead!"

Less than two minutes later Jacob and Catherine saw Raoul step out from behind a tree and motion for them to join him. They hurried their horses to a gallop, and when they reached the hiding place they gracefully dismounted. Raoul quickly grabbed their horses' reins and pulled them into the opening of the thicket.

"What's wrong, Raoul? Did you see any guards?" whispered Catherine nervously as she ducked into hiding.

"Not yet, but there are fresh horse tracks that bear Humphrey's seal all around."

"From the sound of the river we must be nearly there," responded Jacob, ready to move on with the task.

"The riverbank is just on the other side of these bushes here. From over here you can see the boulder," answered Elizabeth nervously. "You'll need to be careful."

She was standing about ten feet away, peering through a break in a natural hedge along the bank of the river. The others joined her.

"It's shaped like a giant frog," Jacob noticed as he glanced at the large boulder he was supposed to stand on.

"Forget the rock. Look at the water—that's far too dangerous!" exclaimed Catherine.

The joining of the Kelbeck and the Upper Stanbourne created a roaring cascade of white water that was hundreds of feet long and nearly eighty feet wide. Near the center of the river at the exact point where the two tributaries came together was the large boulder. Dangerous rushing water lapped violently against its sides while racing to reach the lazy, meandering stretches of river downstream.

"How will you reach it?" asked Catherine. "It is completely surrounded by those violent… Can you even swim?"

"I don't know. I've never tried," answered Jacob with a smile. "I'm just glad that this task requires moving horizontally and not vertically. Besides, I don't plan on getting wet. I'll jump from rock to rock until I get there."

"That's the only possibility," Raoul agreed, "but even that won't be easy. Some of those rocks are not only spaced very far apart, but they are likely to be slippery. A few of them might even be too unstable to stand on."

"Well, you three stay here and avoid being seen. I'm going to find that cave. It won't help to just sit here and worry about it."

CHAPTER 31

As Jacob stood at the side of the river before him, he quickly decided that it was best to concentrate on one rock at a time. The first few were not very far apart and still in fairly calm water. The next three or four would require the use of all of his lion abilities.

There was no way, he realized, that an ordinary person could reach the large boulder without getting wet, or killed. *I wish I could trade my sight for flight right about now.* Jacob stepped off the riverbank and onto the first rock in front of him. *One*, he thought, counting his progress.

Pushing off hard with his left foot, he easily reached the second rock with his right. It moved slightly but settled back into its normal position as he set his left foot down and swung his arms quickly to gain his balance.

Two.

A frightened fish darted quickly upstream. Jacob paused briefly and surveyed the next rock that was four or five feet away. It was small and barely sticking up above the surface of the water. Realizing that there was no way that he could stop and stand on top of the small rock, Jacob pushed off again with his left foot, landed solidly on the small rock with his right, and then instantly propelled himself forward again. Just to show off for the others, who were watching his every move, Jacob completed a graceful flip and landed expertly on top of a solid flat rock nearly one third of the way across the river.

Three, four.

Jacob glanced behind him to see his progress and then smiled in the direction of his companions' hiding places. He couldn't see the others but had a feeling that he would later be chastened for that last trick.

Jacob was now completely surrounded by rushing water, and the roar of the churning river was deafening. Looking ahead again, he guessed that the next rock was at least twenty feet away.

Forget this one at a time thing, Jacob thought.

In order to get as much momentum as possible, he backed up to the rearmost edge of the flat rock, took two long strides, and bounded forward, pushing off hard with both legs at the same time. Arching high over the rapids below, he landed gracefully on his intended target and sprung without pause toward the next river stone. As soon as his feet touched the rigid rock, he leapt powerfully to the next and then the next and finally found himself standing on the frog-like boulder.

Remembering his task, Jacob climbed to the highest point of the boulder beneath him as he recited the latest words from the sword's inscription.

Go to where the waters join and stand atop the polished stone,

A northward gaze reveals a clue that none can see but you alone.

Focus well to see the crag and on it find the piscine cave,

It can't be seen without the sight the little golden raptor gave.

Looking down at the rock beneath him, Jacob saw a weathered arrow carved into its surface. It pointed just slightly west of straight north. Straddling the arrow with his feet so that they were parallel with the arrow's shaft, Jacob concentrated intently on the mountains in the distance. He had been practicing his newest skill since leaving Woodhurst, but these snowy peaks were farther away than anything he had tried to focus on before.

As Jacob peered into the distance, he watched the cold waters of the Stanbourne River flow out of the mountain range as they rushed away from the distant source—the icy waters of Lake Ocktarn. Jacob shivered as he thought about how cold the water thrashing all around him must be.

Jacob redirected his gaze to a mountainside just slightly to the west of the cascading waters. *The arrow is pointing right there, but I don't see anything that looks like a cave.*

It was too far away. Jacob focused harder. Suddenly a familiar wave of dizziness began to emerge from deep inside Jacob's head, and an instant later the hillside enlarged into clear sight. Previously bunched clumps of green became separate and distinct evergreen trees. Boulders were sharp and crisp and as large as could be, and shadows formed by clouds above danced as they swept across the mountain's slope.

That shadow isn't moving, thought Jacob as he concentrated on a particular dark shape higher on the hillside.

"That's it!" he yelled with excitement. "The piscine cave!"

His words were drowned out by the roaring rapids around him. Jacob could now clearly see the dark outline of a jumping fish set into the side of the mountain. Below it was a rocky overhang and a steep drop off into a quarry of jagged rocks . The usual dizziness returned as the mountainside zoomed back out of sight.

This just gets more and more difficult at every turn. Jacob closed his eyes and regained his balance. It returned quickly this time.

Jacob quickly leapt from rock to rock as he hurried back across the river. After his feet touched the comforting grassy ground of the river's edge, he rushed toward the clump of trees that served as the hiding place for the others.

Stepping off of the path and into the shadows, he said, "Well, we go north."

"I don't think so. The dungeons are the other way," came a surprising reply.

"Run, Jac—" yelled Catherine before a dirty hand covered her mouth roughly.

CHAPTER 32

Jacob jumped back quickly and unsheathed his sword in one smooth motion. Even as it emerged from the scabbard, the brilliant blade began to glow intensely. Instantly the profound brightness cast away the shadows all around Jacob and brightly lit up the clump of trees.

Jacob clearly saw four wide-eyed guards standing before him, all with swords drawn. One of the men stood directly in front of him, while the other three stood behind Catherine, Elizabeth, and Raoul, each with a sharp blade held beneath their chins. Catherine's mouth was still covered, but she was wriggling and struggling as much as she dared with the sword at her neck.

"Unhand them right now, and I will let you all live," yelled Jacob ferociously.

The sword grew even brighter. The guard holding Catherine took his hand away from her mouth, but none of their swords moved.

"There's only one of you, and there are four of us," replied the guard in front of Jacob. He sounded less confident than he should have considering the odds.

"Unhand them or suffer the consequences!" Jacob saw Raoul's captor loosen his grip slightly, and his eyes grew wide with fear.

"There's a gold reward for your capture, dead or alive, and the return of the princess, and I intend to collect on it," replied the nervous guard who was doing all of the talking.

"Sorry to disappoint you, but gold is the least of your worries right now." Jacob slowly raised the glowing sword to eye level and pointed it directly at the man.

The man took a small step backward.

"Now!" yelled Raoul loudly as he grabbed the right wrist of the guard behind him with both hands and twisted with all his might.

The startled guard's sword fell free as his forearm snapped loudly. He groaned with pain as Raoul flipped him head over heels onto the hard earth.

Jacob sped forward. He swept his brilliant sword swiftly toward the left side of the guard in front of him. Just before impact he turned the blade mercifully so that the flat side struck with a heavy thump into the man's hipbone. Jacob felt the bone crush beneath his blow and heard the man moan in agony. He joined his fellow guard on the rocky ground.

Jacob then lunged toward the man holding Catherine. The guard dropped his sword, pushed Catherine to the ground, and fled as quickly as he could. He ran headlong into the thicket behind him, covering his head with his arms as the branches tore at him from all directions. Seconds later the sound of breaking branches ended with a scream and a splash as the frightened man fell forward into the icy cold river.

After spinning around to help his mother, Jacob saw that the fourth guard was already lying on his back with Raoul's foot on his chest and the point of his own sword at his neck.

Jacob rushed over and helped Catherine up off of the ground. "I'll be right back. We can't let the wet one tell the other guards." He sheathed his sword and left the suddenly gloomy hiding place in Raoul's capable hands.

"Let's get them tied up then," Raoul suggested as he corralled the embarrassed and injured royal guards into the center of the thicket.

"No, dear, let me help them," offered Elizabeth as she began tenderly caring to the guards' injuries.

Over the next few minutes Elizabeth expertly set and splinted the guard's broken forearm with sticks and rope and helped position the man with the shattered hip against a tree trunk.

"I'm afraid I can't do much to help you, sir, but the physician in Strathwick is a good friend of mine, and I have no doubt that he can make you well," Elizabeth said softly.

Raoul handed the man a sturdy branch that he could use as a walking stick.

"Why did he turn the sword?" questioned the guard as he lay against the tree. "'He could've cut me clean through."

"Because Jacob's a good and honorable man," replied Catherine. "He didn't steal anything, and he didn't kidnap me. I wanted to leave."

"Why does his sword glow, and how does he move so quickly?" questioned the third guard, who had been silent until now.

No one answered at first. Finally Elizabeth spoke, "Sir, you might as well know. That is the sword of King Rowland, Jacob's father. It's a powerful weapon when borne by a worthy heir to the throne. Your lives have been spared by the rightful king of Avondale. Choose carefully where your loyalties lie, or you may find yourselves on the wrong side of this conflict."

"But how does he move so quickly?"

"His friends' lives were in danger," answered Raoul, wondering if they had already said too much. "There was nothing more to it than that." After a pause he added, "But you would do well to follow my wife's advice. Word is already spreading about Jacob and his future rule over Avondale. I would suggest that you seek the healer in Strathwick, but say no more about what has happened here for the time being. Ambrose would not be pleased with you if he were to find out that you've failed him."

"No, sir. He sure *wouldn't* be happy. I for one won't say anything," agreed the guard with the broken hip. He stared at the other two guards until each of them nodded quietly.

"Hopefully this one won't talk either," said Jacob as he pushed his sopping wet captive back into the dim thicket. "He nearly drowned while trying to get away." As Jacob stepped in behind him, the two guards quickly moved to one knee and bowed their heads.

"I th-thought I c-could escape if I crossed the river," explained the wet, shivering man. "B-but the water is so c-cold and fast and I w-went under."

"I jumped out on a rock and grabbed him as he drifted by," Jacob said in order to explain why he was still perfectly dry.

Noticing the guards kneeling before him, Jacob looked at Catherine in confusion. She smiled.

Elizabeth quickly retrieved a blanket from her horse pack and wrapped it around the shivering man. "After we leave, please wait at least an hour before lighting a fire. We'll need a head start to avoid the other guards."

"Yes, ma'am," replied the four guards together.

Jacob and the others traveled back along the south bank of the Kelbeck Brook until reaching the Beckford Bridge. They only dared pause long enough to replenish their water supplies and their horses with the refreshing water before starting up. They were under constant fear of being discovered again and knew that if there was a next time they could be severely outnumbered. Raoul was concerned that the guards they had left behind might tell the others what had happened and that Jacob had headed northward.

"I hope we did the right thing by letting them live," said Raoul as he mounted his saddle. "We should have at least tied them up."

"What if nobody was to find them?" questioned Elizabeth, who was already in her saddle. "It would have been more compassionate to just kill them quickly than to leave them tied up without food, protection, or warmth."

"I just hope they will be honorable men," Raoul said. After crossing the bridge, the travelers rode quickly for many hours, eventually reaching the foothills of the northern mountains where they found refuge for the night. They had covered many more miles than was typical for a single day, but they had felt a strong need to get as far away from Aberfield as possible. As dusk was approaching and the setting sun falling quickly toward the western horizon, Jacob climbed a small foothill and scanned the surrounding area for royal guards. He didn't see a single person in any direction for many miles around, and even Raoul relaxed at the news. Everyone received some much-needed and well-deserved rest.

The following morning Jacob provided a breakfast of wild berries and roasted stag, and the revitalized group traveled quickly eastward toward the location of the piscine cave.

As he rode, Jacob thought back over the long days that had passed since he and the others left Raoul's cottage in the forest. The weather had been mostly pleasant and cooperative, but summer was approaching, and the days were getting warmer. Their bodies had become accustomed to the long hours of riding and the rationing of food and water. Profound weariness made it easy to sleep on the hard earth each night, yet he longed for the comforts of the castle that he had always taken for granted.

A few hours later, even Mabel was beginning to show signs of weariness, so Jacob slowed her to a walk and allowed the others to catch up and ride alongside.

"We would be there by now if we hadn't taken such a long route around Aberfield," said Catherine with a tired voice.

It was nearing late afternoon, and this was the second day in a row that they hadn't stopped for a midday meal.

"A necessary precaution," answered Raoul quietly.

His horse seemed to be the most exhausted of them all, and he reached forward and patted him gently on the neck. He felt much warmer than usual and was sweating profusely. They had given the last of their water to the horses more than an hour before, but it hadn't been much, and his horse was clearly dehydrated.

"We're almost to the river, boy," he whispered. "I hope."

They rode slowly now, all side by side, giving their weary horses a much needed break from galloping.

A short time later Elizabeth exclaimed, "I think I can hear it!"

Instinctively, everyone stopped and listened for the sounds of the cascading river up ahead. It was faint but unmistakable.

Even the horses seemed to sense the nearness of the thirst-quenching water, and without needing to be urged on, began trotting forward. The roaring river became louder and louder until the eight weary companions finally found relief from their profound thirst.

As they relaxed along the river's edge and allowed their horses to rest and graze on the lush green vegetation along the bank, Jacob, Catherine, Elizabeth, and Raoul discussed the nearby cave.

"We won't be able to see the cave from below, but I think I'll recognize the area when I see it," Jacob said confidently. "Based on what I remember seeing while standing on the boulder, we should be close."

"How will you get up to the cave?" questioned Raoul.

"I've been wondering the same thing. From what I could see, the face of the rock was too flat to scale, and a fall from the cliff into the jagged rocks below would mean certain death."

"You'll need to approach it from above," Elizabeth suggested. "If the overhang is as you described it, it seems impossible to climb up from the bottom."

"That's a great idea." Raoul walked over to the horses. When he returned to the others, he was holding many long sections of thick, sturdy rope. He began tying them all together with strong knots. "There should be plenty of rope here to lower you down slowly onto the ledge. You and I can go to the cave while the women watch the horses."

"I'll make sure that no one is coming." Jacob stood and climbed a small hill that gave him a better view of the valley below. After a minute or two he returned and said, "I don't see a single person between us and Aberfield. The women will be fine if we go now."

Raoul stood and picked up the long knotted rope.

"We'll be back soon. You two should rest," said Jacob.

"I won't argue with that," answered Catherine, "believe it or not."

CHAPTER 33

"That's it. There," said Jacob as he pointed to rocky shelf jutting out from the side of the mountain. "I know we can't see the cave, but I am sure that it's there."

"We'll go up the trail a little farther and then approach the cave from above."

Soon Jacob and Raoul were standing on a side hill directly above where they guessed the cave would be. Straight above them was a single tree that was sturdy and strong.

"That can't be a coincidence. This tree was planted here years ago," Jacob guessed.

"It was probably planted here for you or for whoever put the figurine down there in the first place," agreed Raoul as he tied one end of his knotted rope to the tree trunk.

He pulled on the rope to test both his knot and the strength of the tree. The tree didn't budge, and the knot cinched even tighter around the thick trunk. Raoul threw the coiled rope as hard as he could, and as it unwound in the air the loose end disappeared from sight.

"I'll stay here so I can pull on the rope if you need me to. Straddle it with your feet as you hold onto the rope and walk backwards."

The dry dirt and loose rock beneath his feet made Jacob nervous as he slowly walked backward down the mountainside. After twenty yards or so, he reached the point where he had to put all of his trust in the rope. The slope transitioned into a vertical cliff, and Jacob was forced to slide down the rope slowly, using the knots to slow his descent with his feet and hands. He was nervous but trusted in Raoul's rope skills and realized that even in this task his lion abilities were helping him .

After descending straight down for at least thirty yards, Jacob found his feet on solid rock and let go of the thick rope. Just as he guessed he would, he found the cave to his left. It was much larger than he had anticipated, but Jacob was glad to see that it wasn't cut very deep into the mountain. In fact, the late afternoon sun illuminated the entrance of the chamber quite well, and even the back wall of the cave, although darker and shadowed, was still visible.

Jacob had only walked forty feet into the cave when he reached the back wall, and except for one small hole directly in front of him, the rock was smooth and flat as it sloped from the floor upward over Jacob's head and met up with the hillside at the top of the cave's entrance.

With a little apprehension, Jacob reached forward and stuck his hand far into the hole in the rock. He imagined something hiding deep in the hole biting him, like a huge spider or a bat, and he quickly pulled his hand out of the hole.

"There must be a long stick that I can shove in there to frighten anything that might be waiting for a fleshy meal," Jacob murmured as he glanced around the cave. Unfortunately, he saw nothing around but dirt and gravel.

After taking a deep breath, Jacob reached his hand in again. The hole kept going farther and farther into the rocky mountainside until Jacob was standing on his tip toes with his right cheek pressed against the smooth rock wall and his arm all the way in up to his armpit. He felt his fingers touch something soft and again jumped back, jerking his hand out of the dark hole. His heart was pounding as he wondered what kind of creature he had just touched and how sharp its teeth were.

What am I doing? Jacob thought. *How can I be so dense?*

He quickly unsheathed his sword and concentrated on making it glow. In the past, the blade would light up automatically as he became upset or angry in battle, but somehow Jacob knew that he could control it. He just needed to concentrate.

Closing his eyes tightly, Jacob held the hilt firmly with both hands and said, "Glow."

Opening his eyes, Jacob was disappointed to see that the brilliant blade shimmered slightly in the darkness but produced no light from within.

Jacob tried again. "Glow!"

Still, nothing happened. Frustrated but not surprised, Jacob closed his eyes again and thought back on the times the sword had illuminated, seemingly on its own—in the grove as Piers and Gerard tried to attack Raoul, at Woodhurst when Catherine called to him while being attacked by the goshawk, and near Aberfield when the guards were threatening Catherine and his mother and Raoul.

Each time he had drawn the sword in order to save someone he loved. He reflected on Catherine, Elizabeth, and Raoul and how much they meant to him. He thought of the other castle servants, who had raised him and treated him so kindly throughout his life. He remembered Ossian, who had helped with his escape and was now being held in the awful dungeons beneath the castle. He thought of the people throughout the kingdom who were burdened with heavy taxes and living in hunger and poverty.

As Jacob stood there, eyes closed, thinking of his friends and fellow countrymen, a profound warmth came over him. He felt an overwhelming love for each of these people and a strong desire to rescue them from their current conditions of hunger and sorrow and pain. As Jacob felt this need to liberate his people, the people of Avondale, he realized that he could sense a bright light surrounding him, even through his closed eyelids.

Jacob slowly opened his eyes and saw that the cave was lit up as brightly as the thicket and the grove before it. He focused his attention on the sword and willed it to form a beam of light that would shine directly out of the end of the blade. To Jacob's surprise, it worked. He held the sword parallel with the floor of the cave and pointed the beam of light directly into the hole in the rock. Deep in the hole he could clearly see a small and supple leather pouch.

Reaching his arm in again as far as it could go, Jacob felt the pouch with his fingertips and was able to pinch it between two of his fingers just enough to pull it toward him and retrieve it from the fissure. He placed the entire small leather pouch into the silk one around his neck, sheathed his sword, and exited the cave. With his spirits high, he easily climbed the thick, knotted rope and was soon smiling broadly as his head came into Raoul's view.

"I see from the expression on your face that you found it," Raoul said, looking relieved.

Hand over hand, he pulled on the sturdy rope and helped Jacob reach the base of the tree. After Jacob released his grip on the rope, Raoul untied and coiled it up expertly, flinging it over his left shoulder.

"Everything went okay, then?"

"Yes, sir," replied Jacob. "Only two more to go."

Raoul slapped the future king on the back and then wrapped his thick arms around him, hugging him so tightly that Jacob was forced to hold his breath.

Perhaps someday he will see me as his son, Jacob thought.

Only when Raoul's embrace slackened and the two men backed up and smiled at each other did Jacob realize that he had been holding his breath for well over a minute. He hadn't even felt the least bit concerned about needing to breathe the entire time.

"I think I know what skill the fish has given me," said Jacob as they turned and walked back toward the path that would lead them to Catherine and Elizabeth. He inhaled deeply and held his breath as he continued walking next to Raoul.

"This should be fun," Raoul said through a wide grin.

"So you didn't breathe the whole time you were coming back down the mountain?" questioned Catherine with a look of unbelief.

"I watched him. He really didn't," Raoul answered on behalf of the slightly red-faced future king. Raoul was doing all of the talking, since Jacob was still showing off his new ability.

"So you mean to tell me that you can hold your breath for more than fifteen minutes?" she asked.

Jacob still didn't answer, but his eyes were starting to water a little.

"Well, that's not a fish skill! Fish don't hold their breath underwater!" Catherine said.

Jacob exhaled loudly. After breathing in again, he said, "Well, whatever long-lost relative of mine enchanted the sword and figurines in the first place must not have wanted me growing gills. It seems that being able to hold my breath will be helpful in obtaining the next figurine."

"Let's read the next inscription," said Elizabeth as she pointed to the sheathed sword at his side.

Jacob removed the silk pouch from around his neck, pulled out the smaller leather sack, and opened it carefully. After turning it upside down and shaking it gently, the expected fish figurine fell noiselessly onto Jacob's left hand. After handing the old leather sack to Raoul, he placed the silk one back around his neck.

Jacob then removed the blade from the scabbard and turned it over so that the coat of arms was facing upward.

"What sound does a fish make?" Catherine asked as the four adventurers stood over the unsheathed sword in anticipation.

No one bothered to cover their ears.

Jacob turned the figurine over so that the head and tail were facing the proper direction and set it down in its intended position. Just as the two times before, the golden figurine and the sword became one. This time no sound was heard.

"Well, that wasn't nearly as exciting as the lion and the hawk," stated Raoul. As the inscription appeared, he read it aloud.

Northward you will find the source from whence the icy waters flow.

Immerse to depths where creatures live, yet man has not been fit to go.

A box you'll find of precious ore, untarnished by these many years.

Inside you'll see the thing you seek and gain the gift of lupine ears.

"Ocktarn it is, then," stated Raoul, confident that he understood the next part of their quest. "Looks like you'll be holding your breath after all." He began readying the horses for departure.

"Lupine ears?" questioned Jacob with worry as he reached up and touched his own. "I'm quite happy with the way they are now."

Elizabeth and Catherine began laughing together.

"Lupus is Latin for wolf," explained the former queen with a smile. "Wolves have a very keen ability to hear."

"You don't *actually* have a lion's mane or a raptor's beak, do you?" teased Catherine. "Although your lips do look a little fishy now that you mention it." She laughed so hard that she bent over and accidentally snorted.

"It sounds like you have gained an animal skill also," said Elizabeth after catching her breath and wiping the tears from her eyes.

"She sure has," added Jacob quickly. "What's the Latin word for pig?"

Catherine stopped laughing.

CHAPTER 34

"There's a rumor going around the kingdom, Your Highnesses," Ambrose said nervously as he and two other guards stood before the thrones of King Humphrey and Queen Millicent.

"Spit it out, then!" bellowed the king. He felt particularly irritated this afternoon for some reason.

"Yes, get on with it. What do you have…to say? Can't you see…that we are…very busy?" questioned Millicent between swallows of something chewy and sticky.

"Yes, Your Majesties," replied Ambrose, who was both frightened and disgusted at the same time. "The peasants are speaking of a new king who seeks to gain your throne." Ambrose winced after speaking the words. He was waiting for a thunderous response, and he wasn't disappointed.

"Jester!" roared the king with such a voice that it seemed as if all of the people of Avondale probably heard him.

"Yes, sire," came a timid reply from behind the king's royal chair. The smallish man with a grotesquely deformed hand stepped into view and bowed before Humphrey. "I'm here, My King."

In a slightly quieter voice, the king asked, "What do you know about this rumor?"

"Not very much, I am afraid, Hum—*King* Humphrey," the jester replied. "When I was last in Strathwick I heard whisperings, but that is all."

"I have heard a name," interrupted Ambrose impatiently. He had no love for the jester.

"Well, why didn't you say so!" yelled the king. "Who is it then?"

Ambrose paused and braced himself for the worst. "Jacob… Jacob of Avondale."

"What? The servant boy who stole my gem?" It seemed as if the walls were shaking. The guards on each side of Ambrose covered their ringing ears. Ambrose wanted to cover his also, but he knew better. Many a king this angry had punished people for doing less.

"And kidnapped your only daughter...or have you...forgotten?" questioned the Queen with a roasted turkey drumstick in her hand.

"Well, yes, there is that, too," answered the king softly while rolling his eyes at the jester, who had begun rubbing his crippled hand at the very mention of the priceless gem.

"They are saying he is the rightful heir," Ambrose explained. He expected an immediate rebuttal but was surprised to see an obvious look of concern flash across the king's face as his eyes met the jester's .

It was the jester who spoke first. "That's impossible. King Rowland died before having any children, and Queen Mary hasn't been heard from since the funeral. And besides that, that wretched servant is only an orphan." His words lacked conviction.

Ambrose saw uncertainty flash across the king's countenance for a second time. The queen stopped chewing, briefly.

"There will be no trial for this criminal. He is guilty of thievery and treason!" yelled the king, who was suddenly back to his old self again.

"And kidnapping," added the queen flatly.

"And kidnapping. He is to be killed on sight! Tell the guards and all of the people of Avondale that whatever man brings this Jacob to an end will receive a reward beyond his imagination. I will give that man honor, land, and enough gold to last for generations to come."

Ambrose smiled broadly. "Yes, Your Majesty." He turned and strolled out of the royal court.

His men followed behind him.

CHAPTER 35

The smell of roasted venison and the sound of a roaring fire slowly awakened Raoul and the women. As had become customary, Jacob arose earlier than the others and found breakfast. This time an impressive red stag provided them with the sustenance that their bodies and minds hungered for. It was warm and surprisingly satisfying.

"It only lacks broth, onions, carrots, potatoes, some peas, and about a half-dozen spices," joked Raoul. "Other than that, it's perfect."

"It's delicious," said Elizabeth, giving Raoul a look that gently scolded him for being rude.

"As long as we are making requests, you don't happen to have any puddings or pies over there somewhere, do you?" asked Catherine.

"I don't, ma'am," replied Jacob, pretending to be a shop owner. "We only serve fire-roasted stag and water here."

Catherine laughed and replied, "Well then, could I please try some of your finest water?"

"You mean the stuff without dirt in it? I'm sorry , but we are all out of that at the moment."

Jacob and Raoul began preparing the horses, while Catherine and Elizabeth packed up the blankets. They had become skilled travelers, and within minutes Jacob was atop the mare and riding northward along the winding, rocky trail with Catherine, Elizabeth, and Raoul following behind. It would be another long day on horseback, but hopefully before nightfall they would reach their destination. The rhythmic beats of the horses' hooves pounding the earth below and the steady breathing from their large lungs were accompanied only by the sounds of the rushing river that led them to the lake.

During the late morning a thick fog settled over the travelers, making it nearly impossible for Jacob to see more than a few feet in front of Mabel's nose. It was eerie and disturbing and lingered for what felt like hours. Just when Jacob thought he could stand it no longer, a cold, gentle breeze from the north drove the oppressive thickness away, revealing a bright, warming afternoon sun. Even the horses' spirits lifted and they quickened their pace and held their heads higher.

Shadows on the hillsides served as hiding places for patches of snow that struggled to escape the searching rays of the sun. Southern-facing slopes welcomed those same shafts of light and erupted into patches of tiny purple violets, long green grasses, and flowering speedwell. Jacob became keenly aware of the beauty and wonder of the earth around him as he discovered some of the real treasures of Avondale.

By late afternoon Jacob and his companions crested the summit of the mountain. Almost magically, it seemed, the narrow, rocky trail was transformed. Fields and meadows covered in thick grasses, wildflowers, and mosses lay before them. Large clumps of trees, mainly pine and white-barked birch, were scattered about randomly. Winter, still struggling to survive, existed as patches of ice and snow, but it was obvious that summer was slowly winning this semiannual conflict. The small river was winding slowly through the meadow but would soon begin its mad rush to the valley below.

"It's beautiful!" exclaimed Catherine who, along with Raoul and Elizabeth, had caught up to Jacob as he paused to admire the scenery.

"It sure is stunning," answered Elizabeth. "I've been here only once before, years ago."

"We aren't far from the lake now," Raoul said. "Another mile or so, I believe."

Jacob urged Mabel into a run, and the others followed right behind him. The horses seemed to enjoy the chance to stretch their legs, and they carried their riders happily as they swiftly galloped through the beautiful grassland.

"We will be ther' on th' morrow. Midday, sir," reported the rough-looking guard as he sat on his horse alongside Captain Ambrose.

"Then we ride faster!" yelled Ambrose loudly, even though the man was only inches away. He wanted the other men to hear him also. "We have trained royal guards searching all over the kingdom, yet we cannot find a simple boy? How can that be?"

"Ee seems to 'av disappeared, sir," came the timid reply.

"Disappeared? Disappeared?" yelled Ambrose in an attempt to appear as authoritative as King Humphrey. "We'll find that boy, and I will have the honor of executing him myself. Do you hear me?" He hadn't told the others about the reward, and the two men who had been standing next to him in the throne room had been surprised to find themselves locked in the dungeons.

"Yes, sir," came the loud, simultaneous reply from the thirty men.

"Now, we'll ride as fast as we can, and we *will* reach Aberfield before we stop."

Afraid to ask, but wanting to know the answer, one of the other guards apprehensively questioned, "Why Aberfield, sir?"

"Because as far as I can figure out, that's where the rumor began! And if anyone asks me one more question, someone might lose a limb!" Ambrose placed his hand over the hilt of his sword.

The guard didn't know anything about any rumor, but he decided it was safer not to ask about it. "You 'eard th' captain! To Aberfield!" he yelled as he rode away quickly.

"That looks cold," was all that Catherine could say as she and the others stood at the frigid shores of Lake Ocktarn.

It was much larger than she had anticipated. Clumps of pine trees placed here and there prevented her from seeing all of the lake at once, but she guessed that it could hold at least fifty villages the size of Woodhurst, maybe more. The lake was situated in a rocky basin, almost completely surrounded by snow-covered granite cliffs. It was mostly cleared of its thick winter crust of frozen water, but chunks of ice still floated around the edges.

"How will you search the whole thing?" asked Elizabeth. "I know I asked you this the other day, but are you sure that you can swim?"

"Well, since I never fell in the river, I didn't have the chance to find out," answered Jacob honestly. " I suppose that now is as good a time to learn as any."

"I disagree," argued his mother. "Now *isn't* really the ideal time to learn."

"I'm not sure what bothers me the most—the temperature, the size of the lake, or the fact that you can't swim," Catherine said, joining in on the former queen's anxiousness.

"Ladies, Jacob will be fine. He's managed to obtain all of the other figurines up until now without any problems. You needn't worry," replied Raoul. He didn't sound very convincing.

Jacob reached his hand down into the water and was completely surprised. "It's warm!" he cried out.

"Warm?" questioned the others in unison.

Catherine crouched down and touched the water briefly. It sent a shiver down her whole body. "You've lost your mind, Jacob. That is as cold as ice."

Jacob tried it again, but this time stuck his whole head beneath the water. It was refreshing. He wanted so badly to dive in head first. He pulled his head back out, shook it back and forth violently to shake the water out of his hair, and said, "It's part of the magic. I have a feeling that I am a good swimmer." He began removing his boots.

"You'll be *very* cold when you come back out. I'll start a fire," said Raoul as he began looking for wood.

"And I'll get a blanket ready," added Elizabeth as she walked toward the horses.

"I'll need some dry trousers, too, please," replied Jacob, who was now standing there barefoot and shirtless. He still had the silk pouch tied around his neck, and his priceless sword sheathed to his side. He began shivering.

"Well, get on with it then. There's no need to stand here half naked and trembling," said Catherine, blushing.

Without a word Jacob dove into the icy water and disappeared into the deep.

CHAPTER 36

Immerse to depths where creatures live, yet man has not been fit to go. A box you'll find of precious ore, untarnished by these many years, Jacob thought over and over again as he swam along the weedy lake bottom.

He knew instinctively that the box would be in the deepest part of Lake Ocktarn. *That's where I would have put it*, he reasoned.

Jacob quickly swam to the lake's outlet, which was near the center of the shoreline on the southern side, not far from where he had entered the water. Just as he suspected, he was an excellent swimmer. Schools of fish scattered in all directions whenever he approached, but Jacob could have easily caught them if he had wanted, if they weren't so slippery.

The water rushed by Jacob. He swam as if he was being pushed from behind by some unseen force, yet at a thought he could stop and float, suspended in the water without needing to worry about rising or sinking.

Jacob studied the insects that swam and crawled along the rocky, weedy lakebed. He saw minnows scatter, running for their lives when larger fish approached, hunting for their next meal. One fish that swam by must have been nearly two-and-a-half feet long and looked a lot like the fish on King Rowland's coat of arms.

I hope that's the largest fish I see, thought Jacob, nervous for the first time since he had entered the lake.

Jacob swam to what he guessed was the center of the granite basin, turned left, and followed the lake bottom toward the west.

I'll check this half first, he thought.

The water grew slowly deeper and slightly colder as he went, but that didn't bother him at all. What *did* worry him was the darkness that was slowly enveloping him the deeper he swam.

Remembering his sword, Jacob reached down, unsheathed it, and held it out in front of him. He expected to have to compensate for its usual heaviness, but it felt weightless in his hands.

Quickly turning his thoughts toward the people he loved, just as he had done in the piscine cave, Jacob willed the sword to glow with his mind. Immediately the sword grew bright, illuminating much more of the surrounding lakebed than he had expected. Large schools of fish retreated quickly into the shadows, searching for refuge from this strange occurrence.

With the lake lit brightly before his blade, Jacob swam as fast as he could, covering the entire western half of Lake Ocktarn in just minutes. He turned around as he reached the shoreline and hurried back to where he began his search. Then, without pause, he swam quickly toward the eastern shore, scattering nervous fish in all directions.

After another minute or two of speedily swimming and searching the bottom of the lake, Jacob saw something way up ahead shimmer in the light of his sword.

That must be the box! Jacob rushed toward it at full speed.

As he got nearer, he could clearly see that it was indeed a little square container, small enough to hold in one hand, and it looked to be made of pure gold. It was sitting in the center of a large flat rock with nothing else around.

Where are all the fish? Jacob wondered, realizing that he hadn't seen even a single minnow for well over a minute.

Unable to push the thought from his mind, he slowed his forward motion as an ominous feeling of dread poured over him.

Something isn't right. He stopped, swung his feet down below his body, and stood on the bottom of the lake.

Holding his shining sword directly in front of him, Jacob stared intently at the box for quite some time. For some reason he felt as if he shouldn't move an inch.

Suddenly, out of the corner of his eye Jacob saw something very large begin to slither toward him. His heart began pounding, and he almost opened his mouth to scream. He quickly aimed his sword in the direction of the movement.

In the light before him was the largest, blackest, ugliest creature that Jacob could have ever imagined. The huge, horrific animal was partially hidden by a large boulder that at one point, when it was much younger and smaller, it might have been able to hide behind. It had grown to a size so large that only its middle section was kept from Jacob's view. The powerful light was confusing the beast, at least temporarily. It shrank back behind the large rock in an attempt to shield its glowing eyes.

The creature was snake-like in appearance, its long, muscular body covered in glossy black scales. It was coiled and circled around itself so many times that Jacob wondered if it was tied in a knot. It had a single row of powerful fins from its massive head to its muscular, forked tail. A split tongue flicked in and out of the serpent's mouth, revealing row after row of dagger-like teeth.

Jacob and the beast stared at each other for what seemed like an eternity.

I can't hold my breath forever. Jacob mustered enough courage to make a move that could possibly be his last.

He took one step forward toward the golden container while keeping the light shining in the eyes of the giant creature. It bared its teeth menacingly and began flipping its tail from side to side. Jacob was still at least ten feet away from the box. He took another slow step forward. The serpent became even more agitated and began uncoiling its self-imposed knot with an easiness that Jacob found to be quite disturbing.

It's now or never.

Jacob darted forward with tremendous speed, like an arrow released from a powerful longbow. He covered the distance between himself and the golden box in the blink of an eye. He swooped to his left and moved the glowing sword to his left hand. While grabbing the untarnished box with his right hand, he looked over his right shoulder at the same time. The black beast had acted quickly. It was uncoiled and in quick pursuit. It rushed toward Jacob in a fit of anger—teeth bared and nostrils flared.

I hope this thing can't survive on land. Jacob raced back toward the center of the lake. He wondered if at any second he would feel the dagger-like teeth cut into his feet and legs. For the first time in his life, he wished he was shorter.

Glancing over his shoulder again, Jacob saw that he was in trouble. The creature was right behind him. It was gaining ground. He veered sharply to his left and then back to his right. The serpent was forced to react and slowed its chase. Jacob flipped over to his back and pointed the blinding sword directly into the creature's eyes. They were just mere inches away. The massive, black pupils constricted instantly. The dazed monster turned away from the light, pausing slightly in its pursuit.

Flipping back over, Jacob sped quickly away. Relief poured over him as he passed by the outlet of the lake. He was almost there.

He made a wide swing out to the center of the lake, veered left, and rushed straight toward the shoreline. Looking to his left, he saw that the angry creature had slightly closed the gap between them but would never catch him in time.

As the water became shallower, Jacob jumped high into the air, breathed in a huge gasp of air, and yelled, "Get behind the fire!"

He flipped and turned before landing skillfully on the soft grassy shoreline at least twenty feet from the water's edge, facing the center of the lake. He held the sword out in front of his body with his left hand and held the precious box with his right. His trousers were soaked through, and steam rose from his head and body.

"Behind the fire!" he yelled again, a warning that the others had quickly heeded the first time.

"Jacob, what's wrong?" screamed Catherine from behind.

"I'm afraid you'll see soon enough," Jacob replied without turning his head even slightly.

He was correct. In the center of the lake the water's surface began to slowly ripple. A huge black, scaly, serpent head
emerged—first the top of its head, then its monstrous, dark eyes,
followed by wide, flaring nostrils and powerful jaws and teeth. It
inched higher and higher until it was over thirty feet in the air,
suspended by a thick and sinewy neck. A single line of ribbon-
like fins cascaded down its back and disappeared into the lake.

The serpent bared its teeth and shrieked a deafening howl,
flicking its forked tongue at Jacob menacingly.

"I had hoped it couldn't breathe out of water," Jacob yelled
back to the others, still not turning around.

Nobody answered.

The creature slowly swam toward Jacob, who instinctively took
a step backwards. The serpent howled another warning. Jacob
aimed the light from the sword into the serpent's eyes, hoping
that it would have the same effect as before, but the creature
had become accustomed to the daylight and wouldn't be deterred
this time.

Lowering the sword with his left arm, Jacob raised the golden
box with his right. "Is this what you want?" he cried out to
the serpent.

It stopped moving.

"I am Jacob of Avondale, heir to the throne, and this box is
rightfully mine!"

The serpent released a threatening hiss and moved forward
again. It had nearly reached the shoreline.

"Just give it back!" yelled Catherine. "It isn't worth dying over!"

Jacob looked down at the precious box and studied it. By the
light of day he could see the obvious craftsmanship by which
it was made. It had handmade hinges of gold; beautiful, ornate
carvings and inlays; and a lid that fit seamlessly with the base of
the box. The carving on the top of the lid was an exact likeness of
the wolf in his family's royal crest. Next to his sword, it was the

most valuable possession that he had ever held. It was priceless, but Jacob realized that he didn't need it.

Acting as if he was still studying the box, Jacob flipped it over in his hand while releasing the small clasp with his thumb and raising the lid slightly. After a quick shake, Jacob felt something small slide out into the palm of his hand. He turned it back upright, let the lid close smoothly, and reengaged the clasp again with his thumb.

"Okay, then. Have your precious box!" he yelled as he held it high above his head.

The serpent stopped slithering forward and waited.

Jacob threw the golden box as far into the lake as he possibly could, and it disappeared almost noiselessly beneath the surface of the water. The serpent hissed a final warning and dove into Lake Ocktarn after its cherished treasure.

CHAPTER 37

"I'm sorry that you didn't get the figurine," said Elizabeth as she and the others sat around the roaring fire.

None of them wanted to be anywhere near the lake after seeing the sinister, slimy serpent, so they had quickly retreated back to meadows and fields from earlier that day and started another fire. Jacob was still shivering in spite of the dry clothing, thick blanket, and blazing fire. He hadn't told them that he had slipped the figurine out of the box without anyone, or anything, noticing.

"It's okay. I'll just go back and get it tomorrow."

"No you won't!" argued Catherine sternly. "You don't need that silly thing anyway. It almost got you killed!"

"She's right. It's not safe," Raoul agreed while staring at the dancing yellow-orange flames in front of him.

Feeling guilty about not telling them earlier, Jacob reached for the pouch around his neck. "I have to admit, I *am* glad that I don't have to face that thing again," he said as he dumped the wolf figurine into the palm of his hand. He looked up and smiled weakly, .

"You got it? How did you do that?" asked Catherine.

Raoul looked up from the fire and grinned widely.

"I slipped it out of the box before throwing it back in the lake," Jacob explained.

"I hope that thing was protecting just the box itself and not its contents," Elizabeth said nervously, looking for any movement to the north.

"Don't worry. I would have heard it coming by now. Something that large would make a lot of noise slithering through these fields."

No one had to tell Jacob what to do next. He removed the blade from its scabbard and paused briefly, allowing the others to cover their ears. He placed the wolf in its rightful place in the coat of arms and watched as it became one with the blade. A long, lonely howl echoed over the meadow and down the mountainside toward the lower part of the kingdom.

"That must have been heard for miles!" Jacob said. He had been expecting the howl but was surprised by its melancholy mood.

The inscription soon appeared as expected.

The sounds that you hear will be only your own,

The bear you may need to accomplish the throne.

Listen for noise, though it vexing may seem,

It will guide you in finding the last figurine.

"Only one more remaining," said Catherine quietly.

"Yes, but this figurine could be anywhere in the kingdom. The other inscriptions made it quite obvious where we should go," replied Raoul.

"Let's get some rest and try and figure it out in the morning," Elizabeth suggested as she stood and started gathering the bedding. "Things generally seem clearer in the morning hours." They ate a meager supper, since Jacob was far too exhausted to hunt and lay down early for the night. Despite his spent muscles and weary mind, Jacob found sleep difficult to obtain. He could hear field mice scuttling through the grasses and birds in far-off trees chattering one with another. He listened for the sound of an eighty-foot serpent gliding through the soft grasses and wildflowers. It never came. The short, rhythmic sounds of the spring field crickets that normally served to welcome sleep rather than hinder it seemed loud and obtrusive to his lupine ears.

I am going to have to learn how to control this skill as soon as possible. Jacob covered his ears tightly with the palms of his hands.

He slept fitfully on and off throughout the night. Morning couldn't come fast enough for Jacob. He had only one more figurine to obtain—the bear.

CHAPTER 38

"Tell me now and you'll get your reward!" shouted Ambrose to the greedy looking man who sat across the table. This was Ambrose's favorite room, Aberfield's interrogation room.

"I heard four guards talking a few days ago in town. One of them had a broken leg or something and couldn't walk. They spoke of a young man who claimed to be King Rowland's son. They said something about a glowing sword. He spared their lives," said the man as he eyed the well-worn leather pouch in Ambrose's lap.

"That's all you know? A glowing sword?" shouted the captain. "That's not worth a single gold piece, let alone a whole bag full." He shook the supple pouch for effect.

"No, sir, I know where he went. The guards heard him saying."

Ambrose's eyes grew wide with eagerness. This was his chance to capture and kill the servant boy and gain his reward. "Well, then?" he questioned, trying to remain calm and composed. He opened the drawstring on the pouch and poured some of the coins onto the surface of the table. They clinked together melodiously.

"Northward, sir. They went north. Two men and two women."

"North? That hardly helps me at all!" Ambrose was furious. He thought he was going to get some real answers, and all this talk about another man and woman didn't make any sense. "You've wasted my time, you filthy man!" He put the coins back into the bag and tightened the drawstring. "Throw him in the wagon! We'll take him to the dungeons with the others!" he ordered to the other guards in the room.

They strode over quickly and grabbed the man roughly by his armpits.

As the guards dragged the man from the room, he pleaded his case and yelled, "Captain sir! We are in Aberfield. The only thing north is the mountain pass. You can create an ambush and capture—."

His last word was cut off by the slamming of the door, but Ambrose had heard enough. A wide, sinister smile formed on his lips.

Morning had been slow to arrive, but now that it had come Jacob wished it away. He had just barely fallen into a sound sleep, it seemed, when he heard Raoul announce that it was time to wake up. For the first time in quite a while Jacob hadn't already captured, cleaned, and cooked their morning meal. Raoul, who was always prepared, had used a small net in the meadow stream and caught plenty of fish for the four of them to eat until they were full.

The adventurers packed up their things, mounted their horses, and began the single-file trip down the winding mountain trail.

Jacob was alone with his thoughts as they descended, and he turned to his next task. *Not a single clue about where to look,* thought Jacob as he recited the inscription again. *All I know is that I will hear something that others can't hear.*

As he thought about it some more, he realized that even now he could hear much better than ever before. The sounds of the Stanbourne as it hollowed out its course down the slopes to the valley below were now more distinct, but Jacob realized that if he concentrated on one certain sound, it was almost as if it grew louder while all of the other sounds around him became muffled and seemingly distant. He could then choose a different noise to focus on, and it would jump to the surface of his mind, pushing all others aside.

Hours passed as Jacob practiced his new ability, and the sounds of the world around him came alive. Bird songs became clearer and richer; the buzzing of the bees provided a gentle, relaxing drone; and the rustling, wind-blown leaves gave a sense of profound tranquility. Jacob was amazed that during his ascent up the mountain just one day before he had only noticed the river and the sounds of the horses. There was so much more going on around him than he had ever imagined, and it made him feel small and insignificant.

Another hour or so had passed when Jacob arrived at a clearing in which they had stayed two nights previously. Hunger and the need for rest prompted him to dismount and lead Mabel to a reward of green grass and water for her morning's efforts. Soon Catherine and the others had done the same, and before long they were all sitting around the charred remains of their previous fire.

It was a pleasant afternoon, much warmer than the day before. The sun was shining, and a gentle breeze was being channeled down the canyon in which they had been riding all morning. While eating a meager meal, the four adventurers spoke of the latest inscription on the sword and what they would do after obtaining the bear figurine.

"What is that noise?" questioned Jacob suddenly. He could hear a faint, high-pitched sound.

The others all looked at each other and shrugged their shoulders.

"It's getting louder," he said while wincing and glancing over his shoulder, looking for the source of the annoyance.

Soon the sharp, irritating noise became piercingly loud, forcing Jacob to press his hands over his ears.

"Where is it coming from?" he yelled loudly to the others. "I think my head's going to explode."

"Jacob! It's the noise!" yelled Catherine both out of excitement and so that Jacob could hear her. "No wonder the sword didn't give you a hint where to look for the bear. There is only one way off the mountain!"

Jacob jumped to his feet, excited that the final figurine could possibly be this close. With his ears still covered, he focused on quieting the irritating noise. It didn't work. It was too loud. He scrambled over a small hill to his right, looking for the source of the sound and hoping to find a way to make it stop. Catherine, Elizabeth, and Raoul raced after him.

As Jacob approached the river, the noise grew even louder, and he noticed that the wind was blowing quite strongly down the ravine that had been carved out by the river over thousands of years. A sudden gust of cold wind rushed past Jacob as it hurried southward. The piercing pitch became deafening and nearly sent Jacob to his knees.

"It's blowing through something and causing the noise!" Jacob yelled as loudly as he could to the others standing right next to him. He pushed the palms of his hands into his ears even harder.

"I don't hear anything besides the river and a slight breeze," Catherine said to Raoul and Elizabeth in her normal voice. She was trying not to laugh at how Jacob was acting. He was in pain.

"Whatever he hears, it must be very loud to him," Raoul said. He too was fighting back a smile.

"I feel helpless," answered Elizabeth as she looked around frantically. "Where's the noise coming from?"

Jacob strode forward to the river's edge and looked around. At the center of the river was a large, smooth boulder at least fifteen feet tall, and near the top there was a small hole, slightly bigger than his fist, that went all the way through the massive rock. The wind was blowing right through the hole.

"That's it!" shouted Jacob as he backed up to get a running start.

He uncovered his ears and rushed forward, pushing off the riverbank powerfully with his legs. He jumped higher than he ever had before and landed near the top of the boulder, gripping it tightly with his hands and legs. The sound was deafening, and he thought his ears would burst. Jacob immediately covered the front of the hole with his left hand, providing instant relief to his ears, and then reached into the back of the hole with his right hand, searching for the figurine. He felt a long, skinny, carved stone that had been positioned vertically in the center of the opening. Pulling it out of the hole, Jacob removed his left hand, and just as he suspected, the noise was gone.

"It was this rock! It has a slot carved in its center!" Jacob yelled down to the others, his ears still slightly ringing.

He tossed it down to Raoul. Jacob reached back into the opening and felt around until he found what he was expecting, a small golden figurine. After dropping it into the pouch around his neck, he leapt from the boulder onto the riverbank and ran to the others.

"That was sure easier than the last one," Jacob said with a smile, before walking over to a very large rock that was much too heavy for a normal man to lift. Looking over his shoulder, he said, "Bears are pretty strong, right? I don't know what other ability it could be."

He squatted down in front of the rock, reached his arms around it as far as he could, and lifted. It wasn't as easy as he had hoped it would be, but moments later Jacob was standing up and holding the large rock high over his head. After a few seconds he threw it and watched it sink heavily into the soft, grassy ground.

"Not bad at all," he said with a smile.

Catherine, Elizabeth, and Raoul all rushed over and gave Jacob a long embrace. They had been through a lot during their difficult adventure and had accomplished their task of obtaining each of the animals in the coat of arms.

Raoul slapped Jacob on the back, stepped back, and said, "Let's get back to the horses. We need to plan what to do next."

Jacob led the way with the others close behind. As he walked he felt much lighter than usual. A burden had been lifted from his shoulders. He knew that there was still much to do, but he felt nearly invincible, not because of his inhuman abilities, but because of Catherine and Raoul and Elizabeth. They had been with him all along and would stand by him no matter what happened. Jacob had a duty to perform, and it had been written long before he was born. A way had been provided for him to accomplish his task. He would not disappoint the people of Avondale.

After gathering around the fire pit again, Jacob unsheathed the sword and removed the final figurine from his silk pouch. He oriented the bear properly over the coat of arms and paused, allowing the others to cover their ears. When they were ready, he set the golden bear into place and watched it become one with the blade. Now all five animals were a magnificent golden color and sparkling brilliantly in the sunlight. This time something unexpected happened.

Two little bright lights appeared at the very tips of the scrolled leaves beneath the hawk's wings, and they began tracing the ornate outline in perfect unison. Whenever the lights came to an intersection, they split into even more lights and continued on uninterrupted. As they did so, moving toward the sharp talons, they left behind a line of pure gold. In less than a second the leaves changed, and the lights were gone.

A single light then appeared in the shield's center and immediately split into four as the shield, crown, and sword, were also transformed. The lights vanished again. Next, it was the banner's turn. The flowing scroll was altered in the same way, ending with the name of the kingdom, Avondale.

Although the whole process had only taken a few seconds, it mesmerized Jacob and the others, who had moved closer and uncovered their ears, so much so that they were totally unprepared for what happened next. All at once a hawk's cry, a lion's roar, a wolf's howl, and a bear's growl exploded out of the sword and resounded all around them. Jacob nearly dropped the sword as he fell back off of the log on which he was sitting and landed flat on his back. Catherine, Elizabeth, and Raoul were so startled that they scurried off in all directions instantly.

Raoul lost his footing and found himself lying in the center of the fire pit with soot and ashes all over him. Mabel and the other horses, fearing for their very lives, darted down the mountain trail, leaving their riders to fend for themselves.

The deafening animal chorus faded, and with hearts still pounding, Jacob and the others repositioned themselves around the fire pit as they were before. Raoul began using his hands to brush away the cold ashes but soon gave up when he realized that all he was doing was smearing them into his clothing.

Catherine finally said in a grumpy tone, "Whatever relative of yours dreamt up this whole plan probably thought that would be pretty funny."

"Will there be another message?" questioned Elizabeth as she leaned closer to Jacob. The inscriptions always intrigued the former queen.

Jacob held the sword sideways in front of him with the hilt lying over his right palm and the flat part of the blade over his left and waited. As expected, the writing appeared. Jacob read it.

Integrity beats brawn as does honesty too,

More than sight, you'll need justice before your life's through.

Agility and hearing may indeed help you reign,

But leadership and compassion are the true skills you've gained.

This journey has given the prowess you'll need,

In ways that are different than you might have believed.

As Jacob finished reading the last verse of the inscription, the sword was suddenly transformed. The coat of arms faded from its brilliant gold appearance into the plain etched outline that it was before their journey began. The dark blue gem at the base of the pommel took on the look of common, aged brass, and the brilliant, gleaming blade dimmed until it appeared just the same as any other sword. It was still an exquisite, ancient sword, but nothing more.

Jacob felt something inside him change too. He hadn't felt the animals' abilities change him as he had acquired them one at a time, but as they left him all at once the feeling was palpable. He felt a profound loss.

Jacob looked up at Catherine, Elizabeth, and Raoul. Each had tears in their eyes, and he knew that they had understood the inscription and had recognized what was happening.

After a brief pause Jacob stood from the log and said boldly, "Well, we still have a kingdom to overthrow!"

PART III

AVONDALE

CHAPTER 39

"Cap'n Ambrose and th' othe' royal ruffians left for th' no-thern mountains to cap'sha King Jacob!" declared the frail yet animated and nearly toothless man.

He was standing on a wooden crate in the center of Aberfield with poverty-stricken people all around him.

"I heard 'em talkin' bout it and saw 'em gettin ready," he added before stepping off of the crate.

A large, sturdy man took his place on the feeble structure, and the wooden slats bowed beneath his feet. "People of Aberfield! Our king needs your help! He is severely outnumbered and will surely be killed if we don't rush to his aid!"

"But, Isaac, you know we can't defeat the royal guards!" came a voice from the back of the crowd. "We don't have any weapons, and they are much stronger than we are!"

"And they're skilled with the sword and are probably on horse-back!" yelled another man.

"Yes, but we have axes and scythes, and some of us have horses. Those that do can ride ahead of the others," reasoned Isaac from atop the crate. "We will fight for our lives and for our families. We'll fight for our freedom from tyranny and oppression. We'll fight for our king!" he added at the top of his voice.

"For our king!" came a thunderous reply from the crowd.

"Long live King Jacob of Avondale!" yelled the large man.

"Long live King Jacob!" shouted the multitude.

"The horses can't be too much farther, can they?" Catherine asked as she walked beside Jacob down the meandering trail. She was tired, and her knees and ankles were sore from descending the steep mountain on foot.

"I'm sure they have settled down by now," Jacob assured her. "It's been over an hour, and we aren't too far from the base of the trail. We'll find them soon."

Jacob returned to his thoughts as he and Catherine walked quietly on. Elizabeth and Raoul were just a few yards behind.

"I was going to use the strength of the bear to rip the gates from their hinges, the lion's nimbleness to avoid being hit by the arrows, and the hawk's sight to survey the area from miles away. I thought I'd be able to hear the guards whisper their plans to one another or an arrow hiss as it sped toward me. I was even thinking of a way to hold my breath for a really long time," Jacob said to Catherine as he broke the silence.

"You would have been incredible," replied Catherine, not really knowing what to say. "But the sword was correct when it said that compassion and honesty and leadership are the true traits that you will need to rule Avondale as its king."

"That may be true once the kingdom is mine but obtaining the kingdom might be my most difficult task yet, now that I am back to my old self again."

"Jacob," said Raoul loudly, pausing until he and Elizabeth could catch up. "We've been talking, and I am still concerned that we don't have a plan to overthrow King Humphrey."

"What do you think about going back to the cottage for a few days to regain our strength and decide what to do next?" asked Elizabeth. "It is only two days from here, and we should be safe."

Jacob thought about the coziness of the cabin. It provided a roof overhead, a warm fire for cooking and comfort, and enough bedding to sleep comfortably. It *did* sound like a fine idea.

Even Jacob was surprised to hear himself say, "There will be plenty of time for me to rest once the task is complete, and I think the three of you should stay there and be safe and comfortable, but I must go to the castle."

"How will you take it over without being killed?" asked Catherine worriedly.

"I'm still working on the answer to that one," Jacob replied. "Look, we are nearly there." He pointed up ahead, hoping to change the subject.

They picked up their pace and hurried onward, excited to be done with the mountains that were now behind them.

"I'm sure that our horses are just drinking from the river," said Jacob a minute later as he and the others arrived at the trail head. "The sun will soon be setting, so they likely haven't gone far from here."

"Actually, you are only half correct, servant boy!" came a familiar menacing voice from behind a tree only twenty feet away.

Captain Ambrose stepped sideways into view with his sword held out in front of him. He wore a twisted grin as he held two fingers to his mouth and gave a very loud whistle. Instantly, more than a dozen guards appeared from behind other boulders and trees. A few seconds later, another five or six guards came into view while towing Mabel and the other horses behind them.

Mabel was furiously fighting against the ropes that held her captive as three frightened and nervous guards tried to keep her in check. She whinnied and neighed constantly and reared up on her hind legs while thrashing her forelegs dangerously out in front of her huge frame.

"What do you want, Ambrose?" questioned Raoul boldly as he stepped forward and positioned himself between Ambrose and Elizabeth, hoping the evil man wouldn't be able to identify the former queen.

A look of alarm flashed across Ambrose's face as he recognized his old captain's voice. His distorted grin returned when he saw that Raoul was weaponless and severely outnumbered.

"I assumed you were dead. It's been a very long time, hasn't it?"

"Not long enough."

"Well, this may be the best day of my life." The evil captain laughed. "I get to kill the servant boy, earn a handsome reward, and then I get to kill you too just for fun."

"You didn't say nothin' about no reward," argued one of the guards, who was struggling with Mabel's reins.

"Yeah, I didn't hear anything about that either!" shouted another one.

"The reward's mine!" yelled Ambrose angrily. He waved his sword around viciously. "And I'll cut down each and every one of you if I have to in order to get it!"

A heavy silence hung over the band of guards. Jacob could feel a thick tension mounting and wondered if these hardened men were now having thoughts of dissension.

"Now, servant boy, unsheathe that sword of yours," ordered Ambrose as he walked forward a step or two.

Jacob obliged by slowly drawing the ancient weapon from its ornate scabbard and holding it out in front of him.

"I'm disappointed," Ambrose said with a smirk. "I heard that it glows."

"Stop right now, Ambrose!" ordered Catherine. "I'm still the princess of Avondale, and you will do what I say."

"I do not answer to you, Princess. I have orders from King Humphrey himself, and I will be wealthy and famous when this is through." Looking back at Jacob, he added, "That reminds me. Where is the gem that you stole? The king wants it back."

"He'll be disappointed then," Jacob replied. "It's gone."

"Well, no matter. Recovering the gem wasn't a requirement for the reward. The king wants you dead…and so do I!" Ambrose rushed forward at Jacob with his sword slashing skillfully in front of him.

Jacob moved to his right to avoid the onslaught. He felt slow and awkward. "I don't want to fight you, Ambrose," he said as he stopped the first of Ambrose's blows with the blade of his sword.

A loud *clang* echoed off of the mountainside. Ambrose attacked again and again. Each time Jacob blocked his assault with a skill that surprised even himself.

I may be slower and weaker than I was a few hours ago, but this is still an amazing sword, Jacob thought as he swung the well-balanced blade back and forth in defense of his life.

"You're no match for me. I am captain of the royal guards!" yelled Ambrose as he attacked again.

He swung hard from his right. He met Jacob's blade again. He pulled his heavy sword in and then thrust it straight forward toward Jacob's stomach. Jacob knocked it powerfully to the side. Ambrose lifted his blade above his head and then down with all of his strength. Another *clang* reverberated over the onlookers as Jacob easily blocked the blow. Ambrose took a few steps back and paused.

"You may be captain of Humphrey's men, but you are not a royal guard," said Jacob with a newfound confidence. "*I* should know, since *I* am your king!"

"You're nothing but a servant!" Ambrose argued angrily as he rushed toward Jacob again. He swung his sword more desperately but was again stopped each time.

"I'm the son of King Rowland and Queen Mary, and since my father is dead, I *am* the king." Jacob parried the blows with a growing confidence.

Ambrose was tiring and seemed astonished at his opponent's skill with the sword. Sensing that the time was right, Jacob readied for his attack. Ambrose swung his broadsword as hard as he could with both hands from his right to his left. Instead of blocking the blow, Jacob stepped backward. The blade missed his body by inches. The momentum of Ambrose's unblocked sword turned his body slightly, exposing his right side. Jacob swung the flat side of his blade toward Ambrose's shoulder with all of his mortal strength and felt a familiar crunch.

The captain groaned in pain and fell to his knees. His shoulder was pushed forward out of its normal position, and his upper arm hung unnaturally. Dropping his sword, Ambrose reached his left hand up to his shoulder for support. He winced as stabbing pains shot down his arm to the tips of his fingers.

Jacob kicked Ambrose's sword toward Raoul and then stood over his injured opponent. He held the tip of his sword to Ambrose's neck and said nothing.

"Have mercy on me...Your Highness!" begged the defeated man, pleading for his life.

"I will, even though it is justice you deserve."

Jacob looked up at the other guards and was surprised to see that each of them had dropped their swords to the ground. During the commotion of the fight the peasants of Aberfield had arrived, and each guard was surrounded by at least four men, all holding a knife, axe, or scythe as a weapon.

"Thank you, people of Avondale! I am in your debt!" shouted Jacob with a cheerful voice. "You've come to my aid, and I will now come to yours!"

"Long live King Jacob!" shouted the people.

CHAPTER 40

"My king, we have sent messengers to Strathwick. They will ride day and night," said Isaac.

A large bonfire flickered in the darkness, illuminating many of the cheerful faces that had found hope in their future king. Music and laughter rang in the background, making it necessary for those around the fire to speak loudly.

"Thank you, Isaac. We'll leave as the sun rises," Jacob said with an air of kind authority. "What about the people of Woodhurst and Dalcaster?"

"Many from Woodhurst are already in Strathwick, sire. The inns are overflowing, and hundreds more sleep outside the walls at night and await your arrival each day. And I suspect the people of Dalcaster will reach Strathwick before we do, Your Highness."

"How can that be?" questioned Jacob. He looked toward Raoul, who was seated at his right hand.

"I am afraid that is my doing, Jacob," he answered with a smile. "I didn't mention it earlier because I was worried that I acted foolishly."

Raoul told Jacob of his encounter with the people of Aberfield and ended his explanation by saying, "They must have sent couriers right away if they have already reached Dalcaster since then."

"That we did," answered Isaac, eager to explain. "They rode the fastest horses they could find, borrowed fresh ones from farmers along the way, and spread the news as quickly as they could. When they were weakened and tired from lack of sleep, another man would ride in their place."

Jacob rose to his feet, cupped his hands around his mouth, and shouted as loudly as he could, "Good men of Avondale!" He paused until the music stopped and all that could hear his voice were listening. "Please get some rest now. Those who have horses will ride with me toward the castle. We leave at dawn!"

"Yes, Your Majesty!" came a thunderous reply.

Turning toward Raoul, Jacob asked, "Will you arrange for some of the strongest men to use the guards' horses and swords and join us in the morning?"

"Yes, Your Majesty."

"And instruct those who won't be riding with us to take Ambrose and the other guards back to the village and keep them under heavy guard."

"I will, Your Majesty."

"They are to treat them kindly and feed them well, but be cautious that they don't escape."

"Yes, Your Majesty."

"Raoul, my name is Jacob."

"Yes, it is, Your Majesty."

"Arise and follow Jacob of Avondale!"

The cheerfulness from the night before seemed to have faded as weary men with tousled hair and puffy eyes were wrestled from their sleep by Isaac's announcement.

Jacob's unsightly cavalry packed blankets, readied weapons, filled leather bottles with water, and mounted their horses without stopping for breakfast. Soon they were on their way, waving good-bye to those who would stay behind.

Jacob, Raoul, Catherine, and Elizabeth led the way with Isaac and the others following behind.

Reaching down and patting Mabel on the neck, Jacob whispered, "Three-quarter speed now, girl." He sensed that Mabel wanted to run but knew that he would soon be riding alone if he let her.

Mabel seemed to understand and reluctantly set off at a proper pace.

Looking back at the large group of men riding behind, Catherine yelled to Jacob, "There must be at least eighty of them!"

"Seventy-three," replied Raoul loudly. "But we could have had another hundred if there were any more horses."

"Seventy-three won't be enough, will it?" asked Catherine.

"There are still many guards at the castle, I am sure, since Ambrose had only thirty with him in Aberfield," answered Jacob. "But it sounds like we will have plenty of men, untrained as they are, when we reach the castle."

Within an hour or two they crossed the Stanbourne River at the Norford Bridge, rested and watered their horses briefly, and began again.

The sun in the sky slowly arched overhead as the long hours passed by the king and his new army. Then as that same sun fell behind the western mountains the weary men and exhausted horses stopped their march and rested for the night.

"Well done, men!" shouted Jacob to his devoted followers. "We'll reach Castleford Bridge by evening tomorrow. Eat the last of your provisions tonight. There will be breakfast in the morning."

The men cheered.

"Where will you find food to feed so many men?" asked Catherine as Jacob walked over and sat next to her.

"I don't know. Many of them look so frail and hungry, yet they follow me without complaint."

Raoul, who was sitting on Jacob's left, said, "Stay with the men, Your Majesty. I have an idea. Leave the food to me."

"Thank you, Raoul. Take Isaac with you."

"Good idea, Your Majesty."

"There must be three hundred of them, King Humphrey. They seem to be waiting on the west side of the bridge," explained the guard, who was trying not to look in the direction of the queen while she devoured her morning meal. He knew that his glance would turn into a stare if he watched her feed for even a brief moment. The only rumor more popular than that of the queen's amazing eating ability was the new one being spoken abroad—King Rowland had a son…and he was coming.

"I don't care how many there are!" yelled the angry monarch, who was sitting at his end of the long table. "Capture them and lock them up. Or better yet, kill them and make an example out of them."

"But Ambrose isn't here, and we are severely outnumbered."

"Outnumbered?" screamed King Humphrey. "Outnumbered? They are simple peasants! My disloyal subjects! They can't defeat my guards, who are well trained and well paid, if I must remind you, in battle. Can they?"

"No, sire, I am fairly certain that they can't," the guard replied unconvincingly.

"You may wait for Ambrose for one more day," answered King Humphrey, who wasn't so sure himself. "But tomorrow morning you will teach those ungrateful commoners a lesson that their soon-to-be widows and orphans will remember for the rest of their lives!"

"Yes, Your Majesty."

———————✦———————

"Raoul, you are amazing!" Catherine said with wonder on her face as she looked around the encampment and saw the men eating so contently. Night had passed, and as promised, breakfast had come.

"Yes, Raoul, thank you very much," added Jacob with profound gratitude. "You've strengthened their bodies and lifted their spirits and helped me to keep a promise that I shouldn't have made."

"Don't thank *me*, Jacob. I promised the good man that you would repay him. This was the last of his fruits and vegetables from the previous harvest, and we have slaughtered his last two hogs. But he gave it all willingly when I explained that his king was in need. His farm is near this place, and I pray we can reward him soon enough, or he, his wife, and their children may starve."

"We won't let that happen," Jacob promised as he stood and motioned to Isaac.

The large man hurried over and waited for his instruction.

"Please tell the men we leave in five minutes."

"Yes, sire." Isaac replied as he spun around and began announcing their departure.

CHAPTER 41

"Look, Piers! There 'ee is!" shouted Gerard with excitement. "Evryone, 'ear 'ee comes!" he yelled even louder. He hadn't turned his eyes from that road all day long.

Hearing Gerard's announcement, people all around jumped to their feet and began cheering loudly as they saw the large group of men and two women riding quickly toward them with Jacob at their head. Throngs of men, women, and even children tried to rush across the bridge to greet Jacob, Catherine, and the others, and many others swam across the river, not wanting to wait their turn crossing on dry ground.

Piers and Gerard were waving their hands above their heads and jumping up and down, hoping to be recognized by their friend King Jacob, as they had been telling everyone that would listen.

"Of cours' we didn' know 'ee was the king when we tried t' rob 'im," Gerard had been explaining all day long.

Jacob, Catherine, Elizabeth, and Raoul, followed by seventy-three happy and proud fellow countrymen of Avondale, approached the throng of people with wide smiles.

The cheering was so loud that Jacob looked at the castle, wondering if they could hear the crowd from inside. He saw a dozen archers hurry to their positions in the battlements. At least twenty more ran and stood just behind the sturdy gates with nervous expressions on their faces. They drew their swords and readied for battle.

Jacob held up his hand as a signal for his people to stop cheering, and instantly the throng became quiet. His eyes met Gerard's and Piers's, and he winked and waved. Gerard grinned widely and looked all around, making sure others had seen the exchange.

Turning to Raoul, Jacob whispered, "Get the women and children on the other side of the bridge and post twenty men on this side to guard the way across."

"Yes, Your Majesty," he replied and quickly rode off, whispering orders.

Turning to Isaac, Jacob ordered, "Assemble your men in a half circle around me as I approach the gate. Those that can use a sword will be in the first line, and those with axes a yard or so behind them. And instruct them to try not to kill anyone unless they must in order to save their own lives."

"Yes, sire," answered the large man before relaying his orders.

Jacob turned next to Catherine and said, "You aren't going to go with the other women, are you?"

"How did you guess?"

"We need to somehow knock down the gate. Will you see what you can figure out?"

"Yes, Jacob," she answered, excited yet shocked that he hadn't ordered men to carry her off to safety. She led Oswyn away to see what she could find.

"Mother, I lost you once already, and you aren't nearly as stubborn as Catherine—"

"Jacob," the former queen answered, cutting off his request, "I have no desire to fight in this battle today. Please be careful." She kissed him on the cheek and urged her jet-black mare toward the bridge.

Raoul and Isaac, having returned from their assignments, took their positions at Jacob's side, and the three of them approached the sturdy gate. The men from Aberfield followed behind on horseback in two arching rows, and hundreds of men stood behind them, ready to fight for their king with whatever weapons they could find.

"Men of the royal guards," Jacob began, "we don't want to harm anyone. I am the only son of King Rowland and Queen

Mary and am the rightful king of Avondale. I have come to claim the throne!"

The throng of people cheered so loudly that Jacob wondered if the outer wall would simply crumble and fall. He waited for the cheering to subside.

When it did, he said, "I wish to speak to Humphrey and Millicent."

The crowd erupted with boos and hisses at the mere mention of the selfish monarchs. Jacob tried to hide a smile.

When the noise subsided again, a large guard on the other side of the gate replied, "The king has offered a substantial reward to the man who ends your life. Rowland had no son, and you are only a servant. By the way, my chambers need sweeping, and my horse hasn't been brushed in weeks!"

The other guards laughed loudly as the crowd erupted in anger, and Isaac leapt from his horse and rushed forward to protect his king's honor. He was furious to hear Jacob of Avondale spoken to in such a way. Even Mabel reared up on her hind legs and kicked her forelegs viciously. The guards scattered backward, forgetting that a thick iron gate protected them.

"Isaac!" yelled Jacob after Mabel calmed down and stood on all four legs. "Get back on your horse! You'll do me no good if you're dead."

The large man stopped his futile attack and did as he was commanded.

Catherine came pushing through the line of men. Looking at Jacob she grinned and said, "A blacksmith from Strathwick was already thinking about the gate problem."

Behind her appeared four men, each carrying a sturdy iron hook with long, thick ropes tied to their shanks. On the other ends more than fifty feet away were eight sturdy horses, two on each rope, facing the grand city of Strathwick. The men ran forward without waiting for instruction and placed them on the thick bars of the gate. The guards, noticing what was happening, rushed forward and began thrusting their sharp swords through the entryway, hoping to stop the hooks from being positioned, but they were too late.

A loud whistle signaled the horses to pull the rope taut, and firm swats to their hindquarters urged them ahead in unison. The gate creaked. Jacob, reaching down, helped Catherine into the saddle behind him.

Jacob and Catherine and the other mounted men parted and moved to the sides, ready to slip past the iron bars into the open archway when the hinges gave way. The gate creaked even more loudly and bowed slightly.

"Raoul will come with me and twenty more also. We'll stop the archers. Isaac, you take forty with you and cut off the guards before they reach the castle," Jacob instructed. Turning to the rest of the crowd, he petitioned, "Stay here out of arrow range until you are signaled or until the archers have been captured!" Jacob then unsheathed his sword, held it high over his head, and yelled, "Pull, people of Avondale!"

Instantly, a long line of peasants formed at each of the four ropes and began pulling in unison while chanting, "Heave… heave…heave!"

More and more mortar crumbled and fell with every synchronized effort, until finally the rocky structure supporting the massive hinges gave way and the gate came crashing down.

As expected, the guards retreated quickly toward the castle as the mounted cavalry sped through the gate three at a time. Jacob and Catherine veered to the right, hoping to enter the castle through the service door leading into the kitchen.

Suddenly, a dozen bowstrings twanged melodiously, launching fatal, flint-tipped shafts directly at Jacob.

"Here come the arrows!" yelled Catherine to Raoul and twenty others, who followed directly behind.

Jacob pulled hard on Mabel's reins. She swerved quickly to the left. The arrows whizzed past—some of them only missing their intended target by inches.

"They are all aiming for us!" yelled Catherine as she looked back and saw Isaac and his forty men split into two groups and surround the guards, who had been standing by the gate seconds earlier.

Realizing they were outnumbered, the guards threw down their weapons and conceded defeat. Isaac and the others with him quickly dismounted their steeds, picked up the guards' swords, and stood behind them, pressing the points of their own blades into the small of their backs.

"Stay behind them! The archers might turn this way!" the large man ordered.

"They're all aiming at me!" Jacob shouted as he heard the longbow strings reverberate through the air for a second time. "They each want Humphrey's reward." He kicked in his heels and pulled on the reins at the same time.

Mabel angled swiftly to her right.

Looking up, Jacob and Catherine both saw the arrows flying in their direction. Most were going to hit the ground to their left or behind them, but two or three were headed directly toward them. Jacob reached back with his right arm, wrapped it around Catherine's waist, and pulled her off of the saddle, swinging her down and holding her along the right side of Mabel's body. As he leaned forward he heard an arrow narrowly miss as it whizzed behind him, right where Catherine had been sitting.

He closed his eyes and waited for one of the other arrows to pierce him. Instead he heard a loud groan to his left.

"Raoul!" yelled Jacob, as he opened his eyes and looked over to see his dear friend slump forward on his horse.

One arrow had entered Raoul's left side, and another had gone through his left thigh, pinning him to his horse. Jacob flipped Catherine back into the saddle behind him. He reached over and grabbed the hanging reins of Raoul's horse. He quickly pulled him over against the castle wall out of the archers' view and dismounted Mabel smoothly. Catherine jumped down also, and they both ran to Raoul's side.

"Raoul! Are you okay?" questioned Catherine, hoping for any kind of answer.

"I'll be fine," mumbled their dear friend. "Just get these things out of me." He motioned to the arrows.

"He sped up and took the arrows on purpose," said one of the other men who had been riding behind. "I saw him do it."

Jacob began giving orders. "Knock down that door and stop those archers!" He pointed at the door leading into the kitchen.

Ten men immediately dismounted and ran to obey.

"Go up the northwest staircase to the very top!" he yelled after them.

"You, you, and you!" he yelled to the three men closest to him. "Help me get him down from this horse! The rest of you stand guard!"

"Yes, sir!" came their replies as they immediately complied.

The three men and Catherine kept Raoul's body from falling, while Jacob quickly reached over and broke the arrow shaft in half that had penetrated his injured friend's leg. With the help of a few other men, they slid Raoul off the side of his horse, pulling his leg outward and over the broken shaft and lowering him gently to the ground. Blood seeped from the wound until one of the men tore a strip of cloth from his tunic and wrapped it tightly over the injured area. Raoul groaned in pain.

"We may be lucky with this one, Jacob," Catherine said as she examined the arrow in Raoul's side. "It appears to be lodged in his hip bone just below the skin."

Jacob looked around and spotted a man who was still mounted on his horse and said, "Summon the old physician in Strathwick and tell him that Jacob, son of King Rowland, needs him immediately."

"Yes, my king!" said the man as he rode off quickly.

"Sire, we have the archers!" announced one of the men from the battlements.

"Very well!" Jacob yelled back. "Bind their hands and take them to the dining room! Be on watch for other guards!"

"Yes, sire!"

"You four will carry Raoul to the royal quarters and stand guard over him until the physician arrives. The rest of you will follow me."

"Yes, Your Majesty," they all replied.

Jacob, with his sword drawn and ready and with Catherine following closely behind, led the group of men through the service entrance into the kitchen. As he stepped over the splintered wooden door and around the toppled tables and chairs, he was surprised to feel a sense of belonging and joy to be back in the castle. This was where he had grown up, and despite his life of toil in this place, it had also provided him shelter, warmth, food, and most importantly, good friends. Glancing over the counter toward the cooking area, Jacob hoped to see William's round, red face and perpetual grin, but he wasn't there.

"I hope none of the servants have been injured in all of this," Jacob said as he looked back at Catherine with a worried look on his face.

"I'm sure they are all fine," she replied with a hint of hope in her voice.

Jacob led his band of followers out of the kitchen and straight through the small door at the east end of the royal dining room. Just as they entered, he saw his other men herding the bound archers into the room through the main doors.

"This is all of them, Your Majesty," said one of the men from Aberfield. "It's strange, but we haven't seen any other guards in the castle."

"Well done, men. Sit them on the floor in that corner over there and leave a few men to stand guard . The rest of you will please go open the main castle doors and bring Isaac, our other men, and their prisoners here."

"Yes, sire," they replied before marching out of the room.

"The royal quarters are just down that hallway," Catherine explained kindly to the four men assisting Raoul. "Lay him on the bed, and please don't leave his side." Looking at the other men, she entreated, "Would some of you go before and make sure the hallway and the room are safe?"

Without a word a group of men ran from the room.

"The physician won't be long now, Raoul," Jacob said to his friend.

Raoul weakly replied, "Be careful. Humphrey isn't likely to just hand you the crown."

The four men carefully carried him out the door and down the long hallway.

"Put them next to the others, and bind their hands and feet," commanded Isaac as he and his men entered the room with their prisoners. Seeing Jacob at the other end, he ran over and said, "Your Majesty, it appears that they have locked themselves into the throne room. Should we cut our way in with our axes?"

"No you won't!" replied Catherine. "Those beautiful doors have stood there for centuries and will be there for centuries to come. You men are always looking to use your swords and axes to break something or cut something down. Why don't we just burn the whole place down? Or better yet, why don't you use a key?"

"We don't *have* a key, Catherine," answered Jacob while smiling. He enjoyed seeing her behaving so enthusiastically.

"We have a key, Jacob! I have a key to every room in the castle," she confessed. "Except for the one upstairs," she added after remembering the secret room on the third floor. "How else would I have won all of those games of hide and seek?" She smiled deliberately, knowing that she had just revealed a special secret.

"You were cheating?" questioned Jacob in disbelief. He began laughing as memories flooded his mind—memories of walking up and down the dimly lit hallways, searching all over for the princess but never being able to find her. "You always seemed to appear out of nowhere, just after I would give up searching." He began laughing even harder.

"I wondered when you were going to discover my secret strategy," replied Catherine with tears of laughter filling her eyes.

"Strategy? That's not strategy. That's trickery!"

"Um, Your Majesty," interrupted Isaac timidly. "The key?"

CHAPTER 42

Jacob turned the large, ornate brass key and heard a click come from inside the ancient lock. He stepped back and watched his men swing the doors open and quickly step inside, making sure it was safe for Jacob to enter the throne room. When they could see that it was safe, they parted to the sides, and Jacob and Catherine stepped boldly into the room, side by side.

Sitting in their usual places on the royal thrones were King Humphrey and Queen Millicent, and they looked very nervous. The queen wasn't even eating. The jester's head briefly appeared from behind the king's throne but then suddenly disappeared again.

"My daughter!" yelled Millicent when her eyes met Catherine's. "Is that you?" she questioned with alarm.

"Yes, Moth— Yes, it's me," Catherine replied.

"Look at how he has treated you. You're dressed in rags, your hair is ruined, and you look even thinner than before!" Turning to Jacob, she added, "This is how you repay us? After years of taking care of you, you kidnap our daughter, and then try and take over our kingdom?"

"Millicent, she came with me willingly, and I have learned that the kingdom is rightfully mine," Jacob boldly proclaimed.

"Rightfully yours?" yelled King Humphrey, who became noticeably worried when no one cowered at the sound of his voice. "King Rowland was my cousin, and I am the ruler of this kingdom," he added with a voice that was softer than usual.

"King Rowland was my father, and my mother, Queen Mary Elizabeth, still lives. You have no power or authority here!"

The jester, upon hearing this news, rushed from behind the throne, ran over to Jacob, and knelt before him. He writhed his crippled hand into the palm of his left hand nervously. After a moment, he begged, "Spare me, righteous King Jacob. Humphrey made me do it. I will serve you for all of my days to right the wrong that I have committed. I was never good at magic. I am surprised that it even worked. I never wanted to poison your father."

"Barnaby!" bellowed Humphrey. Jumping from his throne with a bright red face, he yelled, "How dare you betray me like that!"

The jester turned and glared at his old friend, but without saying a word turned back to Jacob and continued, "He yearned for the throne and promised me wealth."

"Poison?" questioned Jacob softly, ignoring the exchange between Humphrey and the jester. "My father was murdered?"

The room fell silent.

Catherine turned and hugged Jacob tightly. "I'm sorry," she whispered softly in his ear.

After a moment Jacob looked up at Humphrey and said, "You had my father killed so you could be king of Avondale? Then you taxed the people, grew fat with power, gold, and food, and threatened them with death and dungeons. You sat and ate here in comfort while my people starved, forced into thievery to feed their wives and children. You slept comfortably in my parents' bed while my people froze, some even to death. Children cried out because of hunger and shivered day and night, longing for the basic necessities of life. You could have provided them with life-giving fruits and vegetables and meats from your storehouse—and with blankets and clothing and fuel to keep them warm. But instead you taxed them and drove them from their homes. You imprisoned their fathers and left them with no one to care for their needs.

"Humphrey and Millicent, I will labor all of my days to right this wrong. I will become weary and will long for a day of rest that may never come, but I, Jacob of Avondale, take from you the burden of ruling over this people. I relieve you of this responsibility. You may now leave!" He spoke with power and authority.

Humphrey and Millicent jumped to their feet and scrambled away from the thrones as quickly as they could. Jacob was once again surprised to see that for someone of her tremendous size, Millicent could move very quickly.

A raucous cheer echoed throughout the throne room as the men of Avondale who had helped secure the castle shook hands vigorously and clapped each other on their backs. A new era had come to the kingdom, and hope had been restored.

"Isaac, for their own safety, put Humphrey, Millicent, and the jester in the dining room with their former guards. We'll deal with them later."

"Yes, Your Majesty."

"Make sure the physician has arrived and that Raoul is being treated. Then send someone to fetch my mother and bring her to his side."

"Yes, sire."

"Find the keys to the dungeon and release my friend, Ossian. Feed him well in the kitchen and then bring him here to the throne room. I want to thank him for saving my life."

"Yes, sire."

"Tell the other prisoners that each of them will be released and fed later today."

"Yes, my king."

"Search for the castle servants and have them assemble in the drawing room. I wish to speak to them also."

"As you wish, sire."

"And Isaac…"

"Yes, Your Majesty?"

"Thank you."

"Yes, Your Majesty," replied the large man with a smile.

"Catherine, come with me!" Jacob reached for her hand and pulled her from the crowded throne room. She smiled broadly and gladly followed. They ran to the northwest spiral staircase and up the steps to the next floor. After exiting the stairwell, they ran down the long hall, passing Jacob's old room on the left. Moments later they ascended the long, straight staircase leading to the third floor. Jacob's long legs allowed him to reach the top step well before Catherine, so he turned back and waited.

"I'm sure that it will be unlocked now that the gem isn't in there any more," he said as he reached for her hand and helped her up the last step.

"What are we doing?" asked Catherine excitedly.

"You'll see." They ran down the hallway together toward the secret room.

When they arrived at the door the knob turned easily, and he swung the door open and rushed inside. Catherine followed behind and looked around. The room was exactly as they had left it just weeks before. Even the shards of bone from the skull were still lying on the floor.

"Maybe we should pick these up now that we can assume he is a long-lost ancestor of yours," Catherine said reverently. She knelt down and began pushing the pieces into a pile.

"I guess there's time for that," said Jacob as he picked up an old decorative bowl among the antique heirlooms and carried it over to where she was kneeling.

He and Catherine picked up the bony pieces and placed them carefully in the bowl. When they were finished, Jacob stood and placed the bowl on the shelf on the wall where the skull had sat for all of those years. He stepped back and helped Catherine to her feet.

While looking at the ornate bowl, Jacob said, "It seems like it's been years since we stood here at the beginning of this whole adventure."

"It sure does," agreed Catherine. "So why did we come up here?"

"The banner," explained Jacob as he hurried over to the wall. "Help me move a few of these things."

Jacob and Catherine pushed, lifted, and slid a few exquisite pots, pieces of armor, and the large chest of drawers away from the stone wall as far as they could in the short time that they had. After drawing his sword, Jacob held it high over his head and sucked in his stomach just enough to squeeze his body between the back of the chest of drawers and the wall bearing the banner.

He scooted sideways until he was far enough in to reach the rope that was looped over a large iron hook fastened to the wall. Using the tip of his blade, he pushed upward on the rope, and after rising to the tips of his toes he was just able to free the large silk banner that bore his family's royal crest. As the banner cascaded smoothly down from the wall, Jacob caught it with his left hand.

He squeezed out from behind the chest, sheathed his sword and quickly folded up the banner. "Okay," he said with a smile. "Let's go."

Catherine, realizing what Jacob was planning, smiled also and ran from the room toward the long straight staircase. They quickly descended the stony steps and ran back down the servant floor's hallway and over to the spiral steps. They climbed the curved stairs; opened the thick, wooden door; and exited the staircase at the very top. As they stepped out and stood on the uppermost part of the castle, they overlooked the kingdom of Avondale.

Catherine looked down and saw throngs of people both inside and outside the castle grounds and on both sides of the Stanbourne River. They stood side by side and hand in hand. Many young children were on their fathers' shoulders, waiting to catch a glimpse of their new king. Farmers, blacksmiths, carpenters, cooks, masons, weavers, shoemakers, woodsmen—nearly all the men, women, and children of the kingdom had come hoping to see Jacob of Avondale.

Jacob looked at his people, most of them dressed in worn-out clothing and wearing sunken, hungry faces, yet covered in bright, broad smiles. "They haven't seen us yet. Let's give them something to cheer about." He reached up and untied the rope at the base of the long pole bearing Humphrey's banner, and with Catherine's help he began lowering it down.

Someone from the crowd noticed the movement and yelled, "Look! The banner is coming down!"

Applause erupted as the people looked up and saw what was happening.

"There he is! That's King Jacob!" shouted a woman near the main castle doors.

The cheering grew even louder.

When the old banner was within reach Jacob pulled it toward him, untied it from the rope, and threw it over the castle wall. It floated down to the people below, drawing boos and hisses from the energized crowd.

In the meantime, Catherine tied Jacob's banner onto the sturdy rope and began hoisting it into place. As the standard began to flap gently in the breeze, the coat of arms became visible to the people—the lion and bear with their front paws on the shield's sides; the hawk grasping the top with its sharp, piercing talons; and the crown, wolf, fish, and sword on its face. The letters forming the word "Avondale" fluttered in the wind as the banner was raised.

When it reached the top of the stout pole, Jacob tied it off, and the crowd cheered and chanted, "Long live King Jacob! Long live King Jacob!"

Jacob of Avondale turned to Catherine and looked down at her tenderly. Her deep brown eyes were sparkling brighter than he had ever seen as they gazed up into his. Her smooth, soft lips formed into a smile—not just any smile, but her flirtatious smile. Jacob's knees weakened as he smiled back. Reaching his arms around her back, Jacob gently pulled Catherine toward him. He turned his head and bent down as she lifted up onto the tips of her toes. The crowd of people grew silent.

Jacob saw Catherine's glistening eyes close slowly just before he closed his own. Their lips touched. Jacob had dreamt about a moment like this many times before—this was better than he had ever imagined.

The crowd erupted into shouts and cheers, and the people of Avondale began a new chant. "Long live King Jacob! Long live Queen Catherine!"